MURDER IN BATAVIA

A novel
by
Richard Mann

MURDER IN BATAVIA

Published by:

Gateway Books

ISBN 0-921333-68-4

In Indonesia

Gateway Books,
Dwimitra Tata Sejati,
Jl. Haji Soleh 1, No. 1G,
Jakarta 11560, Indonesia.
Tel: (62-21) 536-0548.
Fax: (62-21) 536-0547.

Front cover illustration by Derek Bacon

Line drawings by Van Gabrielse

Inside front cover photograph courtesey of
Royal Institute of Lingustics and Anthropology,
Leiden, the Netherlands.

Major Hugo Van Es stepped out of his personal office in the Commissary complex, pulling the door closed behind him with a sharp gesture of finality. He turned the key in the brass lock with a quick twist of the wrist, slipping the bunch to which it belonged deftly into his trousers side-pocket. Regardless of how positive and productive his day may have been, every afternoon at this time, Van Es was seized involuntarily with the deeply pleasant feeling of 'shutting up shop', of bringing his affairs to a complete, if temporary, termination. After this, his time was his own. He walked off along the wide, airy, corridor whistling softly, thinking already of the delicious hours of freedom ahead.

He had been intensely bored with his job for a

very long time and mess-mates had given up asking him about how his day had been.

"Your problem is that you're too damned efficient for your own good," brother officers joked at the mess bar, whenever something happened to provoke him to moan and groan more loudly than usual about his fate as a desk-jockey.

Momentarily, Van Es's blue eyes would stare sightlessly and he would habitually suck in his breath with exasperation before expelling it noisily to gulp down a large draught of the daily beer which, like everyone else, he found helped him, not only to get through the nights but through the days as well.

"Anyway, you're bloody lucky," his colleagues went on. "A lot us who have to go out searching for rebels in the jungle would love to have your job."

"<u>You'd</u> all think that," Van Es would reply explosively, "until you've tried it for a while. After nothing but negoSititing rice or coffee prices with the Chinese and then having to check and double check every transaction and promise and finding at least half of them broken, I'm telling you, it drives a man crazy! More beer here barman. Cepat! Cepat! (Quickly! Quickly!) for God's sake."

Van Es was still young enough and ambitious enough to be champing at the bit to see action. There was fighting against anti-Dutch rebels in Aceh and Bali, yet the most dramatic event in his day was an unexpected hike in commodity prices or a row with a vendor. Yesterday, in a mood more upbeat than he had felt for some time, he had told them:

"You'll all be pleased to know that I have yet

another application in for transfer to an active unit."

His announcement was greeted by a storm of good natured but irreverent laughter.

"With your luck you'll be transferred from the Commissariat to ordnance," someone said to the company at large.

Van Es cursed and slammed his beer glass down hard on the bar. "I wish I had never learnt to count so damned well."

"You mean you wish the natives had learnt to count so a European didn't have to do the job."

"That, too - if we could find a Chinaman or an Inlander we could trust!"

When he finished work at around four o'clock it was too early to go to the Officer's Mess so, usually, Van Es made his way to his quarters, threw off his boots and uniform and lay down on his bed for an hour or so. Flinging his arms up above his head and closing his eyes, he liked to luxuriate in feeling the stress of the day flow out of him. He deliberately tried to think about absolutely nothing. On many insufferably hot afternoons he succeeded so well that he was soon sound asleep. For some reason he always slept better in the afternoon than he did at night. And there were fewer mosquitoes! It was strange; to him mosquitoes were a mere irritation. To men who went to the front lines their bites could be life or death!

"I don't know what's worse," a field officer had once said, "to fight Inlanders or to fight mosquitoes."

"You can never see either of them," someone had quipped cleverly, sending the bar up in gales of semi-inebriated laughter.

When he woke up from his afternoon siesta, there was the usual anxiety about knowing what time it was, calling to the house-boy to get his mess kit ready, waking himself up even more thoroughly and decisively with an icy douche or 'mandi' and generally preparing for the nightly pre-dinner drinks at the mess, or, sometimes, at the Concordia Club.

The Concordia was Batavia's prestigious Club for senior military officers - soldiers in uniform weren't welcome virtually anywhere else! Sometimes, Van Es could be found at the Concordia, sometimes at the regimental mess. He hated to throw money away by going every night to the relatively expensive Club just to have a drink and a meal similar to the fare available at the mess at a lower price. On the other hand, there were times when it was a welcome break from the inevitably circumscribed talk of the regimental officers mess - talk which if it touched on combat only served to intensify his envy and unsettle rather than relax him.

If one wanted promotion, it was extremely beneficial to be seen at the Club, to be known, to know people, especially influenSitil people, and to keep one's ear to the ground for opportunities. At the Club, one met officers from other regiments and from other levels up through battalion and brigade until general staff. Compared with the mess, the Club was altogether a different proposition. As a matter of operational fact, one had to attend both from time to time - the mess to keep in touch with peers and the Club to find out what was going on in the big picture, to keep in social touch, especially with superiors, and also to try to ensure upward mobility in

one's career.

Promotion was important to Van Es. He had not arrived in the Indies with a cloud over his head or the law on his heels. But he had arrived penniless. It was a familiar story; good family but no money! He had joined the colonial army out of choice because, for a man in his position, it appeared to offer opportunities for fame and fortune - in contrast to the staid, slow, predictability of life in the Netherlands. Good men were in constant demand in the Indies but, equally usually, in short supply.

His posting to the Commissary, though laden with responsibility, had not been his choice. In military service, could it really be said that one ever had a choice? But at least some postings were more congenial than others. What Van Es had had in mind was making his name as a field officer by helping to establish Dutch rule throughout the wealthy East Indies. Instead of the perceived glamour of the gun he had been allocated the tedious and dull work of the Commissary. Yet it was work, like the supply of ordnance and other vital logistical requirements, which had to be carried out reliably and in time. An army without either food or bullets couldn't achieve much! While he thirsted for a job in the field, his superiors sought to convincc him that there was more than one way to the 'top'.

"You understand the importance of regulations and procedures Major. Perhaps fate has decreed that your way must be through the counting house," the Colonel of his regiment had said, semi-jocularly.

Van Es had shot back his famous blue eyed stare but stopped short of sucking in his breath in front of a senior officer.

"We need men like you behind the lines to keep our men fully supplied at the front," the Colonel had said. "You must never feel that we think less of you because you are not in the field. On the contrary."

So, that was the position. Van Es, frustrated and fighting to quit his post - the army very happy with him and doing all it could to stop him moving.

As he said, Van Es had applied for an active service post - which merely signalled to superiors that perhaps the time had come for something more substanSitil than promises and talk to make the Major happy.

"Maybe a promotion and more responsibility in a wider theatre would satisfy him," said the General.

"The promotion would have to come first, sir."

"To lieutenant colonel or even to colonel, maybe. Let's think about it. Perhaps someone can sound him out at the Club."

"I think it's a different job that he'd really like, sir."

"Yes, I know," said the General thoughtfully. That's the problem."

Van Es's mess cronies thought he was mad to want to get out of the Commissary.

"I'd give my right arm and one of my legs to have your job," was a typical response to his nightly complaining.

"Because you all think I make a lot of money on the side but I never take a cent from anyone."

"More fool you," those around him laughed loudly. "Who's ever heard of a commissariat officer without money?"

Yet it was true. Van Es did not sweeten deals with Chinese compradores (finders and fixers) with 'commissions' for himself. He lived on his military salary, like everyone else, a salary never known for its exorbitance! Van Es wanted to succeed following the straight and narrow road, not the crooked and winding one. Fiddling the books at the Commissary was not what he had in mind. Promotion and, perhaps, fame, he felt, should also bring the monetary rewards he sought.

If he had to suffer the Commissary, the main thing was to have excitement in his otherwise humdrum life from some other source. Van Es was a bachelor and should have been living in barracks at the officer's quarters. Although he, himself, had no money, a distant relative, who had also been in the East Indies service, owned a small villa between Senen and Weltevreden which he had won at a game of cards. Rather than have it stand empty, the Major had been lucky enough to be granted exceptional permission to use it. Life in barracks would have been squalid in comparison!

It was a truly charming house, reached through a small front garden, well planted with pines, shady broad-leafs and shrubs. A deep, cool, veranda, beneath overhanging eaves, led into the main living room with bedrooms on either side and servant's quarters at the rear. Van Es kept only one servant for his simple needs, a young Javanese houseboy called Supardi, nicknamed Sup. For a man as lustful after fighting as Van Es and also a man who could be quite as cruel as he was kind, the house seemed oddly artistic. But, then, it wasn't his. He was just the privileged tenant. But being the tenant gave him the one thing he could never have had in barracks - privacy! Van Es was friendly enough when you met him - especially after a few drinks - but there was a part of him that was a loner, a part of him that wanted to do whatever he felt like doing - secretly, unobserved.

Though he worked in an organisation that was almost by definition a collective, an important part of Van Es was intensely individualist. He was, as they say, his own man. Not that he was ever up to no good in his spare time. Far from it. At the Commissary, no one was more of a stickler for the rules and regulations than Van Es. It was just that there were some things which, if done, it was better for society at large not to know about. Colonial society increasingly expected and demanded certain behaviour and, in public, it would not accept any but the highest standards. In some branches of the colonial administration, for example, the law and the security forces, such demands and expectations were at their highest.

Yet men were only men. They possessed natural needs which had to be satisfied - for example, for women. But where were the women and what kind were they? Under certain circumstances, it might have been wonderful if he could have had the pick of a pool of young Dutch women but, in the past, relatively few had decided to make their lives in the Indies. Because of this, like almost every other normal male, Van Es had been forced to look for female companionship among the local girls. Traditionally, officers and other ranks had been actively encouraged to live with native women. Many local women even lived in barracks with their lovers, performing the extra function of keeping the place tolerably clean. And many senior officials and private businessmen with their own quarters had live-in 'housekeepers'.

But there were always double standards. What was good for the men was not necessarily good for officers. What was good for some officers was not necessarily good for others. Generally speaking, the higher up the command ladder an officer was, the further into the background his local companion should be.

Another consideration, from Van Es's point of view, was that a 'housekeeper' would quickly have become indistinguishable from a 'real' wife. But Van Es felt that he was not yet ready for the one woman scenario. Frankly speaking, he liked playing the field.

Many Europeans thought the Inlander girls ugly. Van Es, on the contrary, never tired of their varied beauty, a beauty that, while not European, was beauty no less - and a beauty accentuated by a perceived animal sensuality as wild and untamed as the beasts of the jungle! Anyone who, like him, had tasted their warm abandon in bed would not easily want to give them up. In Van Es's opinion, you couldn't compare an olive skinned, dark eyed, island girl, with her near abject loyalty, willingness to give service, her loving disposition and her radiant smile - you couldn't compare any of this with a white woman.

Van Es was reasonably young, tall, well built,

handsome - if one felt that sun-tanned skin, fair hair, cropped, army-style, and blue eyes were handsome - and, since many of the dark-skinned Indies' girls believed just that, he was in constant demand. Many a raven-haired beauty would have been pleased with even the smallest attention from Van Es.

But the women in his life were no more than that - 'women.' He was not looking for a mother for his children or for a partner who could share his life in European society. For these things he preferred that any wife he might take should be Dutch. All Van Es wanted was a woman and to counterpoint his boring days with the unadulterated fun of his nights! It goes without saying that what unattached European women their were in Batavia would never agree to be part of his 'playing the field.' Everyone knew what kind of girls allowed themselves to be used by men like that!

Tonight, Van Es pretty-well had to go to the Club; he had been invited to make a fourth at bridge. Anyway, he'd been to the mess quite a few nights in a row.

One of the problems with life in Batavia was the very few public places one could go to for relaxation and entertainment. There were the hotels, of course, but these were all relatively expensive. And all were closed to military personnel wearing uniform. It was the same at the Harmonie Club but, in any case, the Harmonie was exclusively for civilians just as Concordia was exclusively for the military. Between the messes, Clubs and hotels and 'the rest' there was a very wide gap after which there were the warungs (food stalls) of the Inlanders or the tea houses of the Chinese.

And, then, like a fantasy-land, there were the places where a man could always find a girl, where there was alcohol running freely, where there were dark corners and secluded rooms for lovers. It was not a respectable world, but, a respectable man could go there, if he was careful. And the mere fact that it wasn't respectable acted like a magnet to some of the respectable! This was Van Es's world after dark. These were the places where, after work, the hours he spent could be called 'delicious'. But one did not go to such places at five or six in the evening! First, one must eat and tonight, he had to play cards.

He had overslept and dressed hurriedly.

"Sup. Sup. Call me a sado (horse-drawn carriage where passenger and driver sit back to back) ," he yelled.

The barefoot houseboy, wearing a white, high-necked tunic and a sarong, with a black pici (round, flat, black hat) on his head, walked with measured treat down the drive to look for one of the little carriages pulled by a single pony. Despite the urgency of Van Es's tone, Sup was not in any hurry. He was Javanese and never in a hurry.

"Cepat, Cepat, Sup," called Van Es, watching his retreating back from the veranda while buttoning his white "tutup" (closed collar) jacket with its high collar.

In this area, there were plenty of sados around and Van Es soon heard Sup's voice calling softly from the garden:

"Sudah, Tuan." ("Here already, Sir.")

Van Es swung up into the rear, with his back

to the driver, and the sado set off at a cracking pace through the streets of the military cantonment. He could have walked because it was not far but he did not want to be too late. He arrived at the Club just in time to grab a single drink from the long bar before joining his party for dinner. The dinner was very civilised, with white, linen, table cloths and silver service, although the fare, being entirely Dutch, Van Es always found a little heavy for the climate. Port and coffee was served at the card tables where the gamblers, more often than not, played, shrouded in smoke from thick Sumatra cigars.

Tonight, in addition to the stress of being late, he mind was on Justina, a new girl he had met, and he played badly. Everyone knew how his relative had acquired his house and tonight he played so badly and lost so heavily that one of his opponents joked:

"You can always bet your house."

"If it was mine to bet," Van Es growled irritatedly.

He was glad when nine-o'clock came and he could say "good night." But he did not go home. He had been looking forward to seeing Justina all day, to feeling her softness near him, to seeing her smile, to entering her world of make-believe which he found such a change from his daily realities at the Commissariat. By now, he guessed she would be waiting for him. She never knew when he would come but on certain nights she somehow sensed that he would, and usually she was right.

Under the thick trees outside the Club, a number of sados and delman (larger horse-drawn carriages) were idling, waiting for late night customers. Drivers called out to Van Es competitively:

"Mana, Tuan?' (Where to, Sir?)

Van Es selected a sado with the spryest looking pony and hopped up at the back.

"Senen," he told the driver, adding detailed instructions as they drove. The pony's little hooves clattered through the echoing barracks-area behind the Club, passed some dark fields, bordered by large trees, their tops thick with overhanging foliage, and eventually came to Senen.

Senen also was a substantial military suburb with barracks, messes, a hospital, quarters, etc., and, in addition, it was the district where Batavia's Eurasians seemed to like to settle. The large mixed Dutch/Islander population was the direct result of the traditional lack of Dutch women in the East Indies. Eurasians worked for the government in almost every department. In selecting Senen, it was as if they were making a statement about their role in the community; they were not fully Dutch and therefore could not expect to live in the premier district of Koningsplein (Gambir) or Waterlooplein (Lapangan Banteng). They were not Chinese and did not want to live close to the old city (kota) around the harbour of Sunda Kelapa. So, they chose Senen, away from the Chinese heartland around the old city and close to the core European settlement and the centre of government.

The main road inland from Batavia and Tanjung Priok passed through Senen, making it a substanSitil junction. Around this cross-roads the inevitable Chinese market had developed, with European offices and European and Eurasian homes stretching out towards Meester Cornelis (Jatinegara). The shops in and around the Chinese quarter were busy until past nine at night but even after the shutters went up, those who took the trouble to penetrate the narrow, back-streets to the west would spy other lights still twinkling brightly from buildings from which could be heard the sound of music and laughter. This was the Senen of the night! Playtime Senen! If being unable to stay away from Senen was a sickness Van Es had it! Whatever they might be doing, men always knew that the girls of Senen were there, waiting, available, tempting, willing, warm and - obedient. The inability to resist their nightly siren calls was tropical sickness indeed!

While he was bored with his job, Van Es by no means disliked his fellow Netherlanders. It was simply that he saw and mixed with their kind every day and he wanted something different. Then there was the fact of being surrounded by men all day - men at the barracks, men at the office, men at the mess, men at the Club. Even at social gatherings at the Concordia, men and women tended to split into single-sex groups! He had nothing against men but he loved the brightness and good nature of women. In fact he loved women, he was interested in women and he liked to be surrounded by them as often as possible.

Any dealings with what few European women were available were, of necessity, very formal. And a man couldn't flit from one dazzling flower to another - as one could in Senen. Then again, European women were part of European society, they belonged to families and they and their families had connections. Frivolous behaviour could soon lead to unpleasant consequences.

He was not alone in his preference for the Indies' ladies of the night, first because there were not enough European females to go round and secondly because many soldiers preferred to 'love' without commitment. Batavia was a veritable paradise for men on the loose and one which many would have been profoundly depressed to have had to give up.

Even if the girls didn't live in, officers and men all knew who had local girl friends and often who the girl friends were. Batavia was a small place and all too often colleagues would bump into each other at some mid-night rendezvous or other. While men in barracks could keep virtually nothing private, Van Es enjoyed a privileged privacy at his villa which allowed him to lead and revel in a virtually secret life. He was not naturally a man to share the secrets of his personal life and none but himself (and, perhaps, his houseboy) knew how many local girl friends he had or what he did with them to pass the time, or where. It was a life which amused him immensely.

In the daytime, he was the efficient, domineering', Dutch 'Tuan besar' (big boss), eager to impress superiors. In the night-time he could be himself; he did not have to give orders to those below; he did not have to watch and check what those below did; he did not have to look constantly over his shoulder to see what impression he was making on superiors. He did not have to feel 'watched' as men in positions of responsibility always feel. A leader, however minor, is on constant public display. In the dark night-haunts of Senen, Van Es was not at all on public display. He could, so to speak, let his hair down with a vengeance, if he wished. Of course, he wasn't totally free. He felt that he still had to be a bit careful with his behaviour around fellow soldiers. But the girls would never spread bad gossip about their foreign boy friends - not to mention paying clients! There were a few places around Senen where a man could drink, listen to live keroncong music and flirt with as many young ladies as one could handle and all with complete discretion.

For the time being, Van Es had taken to going to a place run by Pak Atek. The building stood back from the road in its own grounds, dotted with clumps of bamboo, similar to those in front of the Concordia Club. The roof was red-tiled but the walls were of woven bamboo. In deference to the European clientele, the floor had been paved. Darkness cloaked the place with a special magic, made even more magical by the bright, flickering gas lamps among the trees. The real magic, of course, was the girls. It was only women who could have drawn sane men to a shack like Atek's. Just as the barracks were crowded with men, Atek's was crowded with women. For a lusting man to push his way through them, feeling their bodies brush willingly against him, was a thrill by itself. And each and every one available! In the daytime, by any objective standard, Atek's was a filthy, dilapidated hovel where no respectable person would wish to be seen. But the night hid all its blemishes, just as the dim light inside made every woman seem a flashing-eyed beauty.

Whatever other shortcomings the Dutch may have felt the Inlanders had, they were good at music. They played and sang well and there was always a small group of musicians, amazingly, sometimes playing the latest tunes from Holland. Beer or arak was served from a heavy-duty, wooden bar at one end but, otherwise, all around the big room, bamboo benches and tables were nestled amid high, cosy partitions. How useful those partitions were! In these small, dimly lit spaces, a man could hug a girl as tightly as if life depended upon it, running eager hands over every accessible part of her; even kissing her. In these little cubicles men petted their girls as heavily as they dared in a public place. Music, singing, drinking, soft and obliging women! What a difference from bridge at the Club! What a difference from doing anything at the Club!

Van Es had been attracted to Justina the moment he saw her. Her features were almost European but her mixed ancestry had highlighted with black those parts of a European face which some might consider weak. While her skin was near - white, her hair was a deep black, her eyebrows were black, and the pupils of her eyes were black and huge against their whites. She combined the dark beauty of the Inlander with the pale sculpting of the European. It was no surprise to Van Es to learn that her father had been Dutch.

During the first few minutes of their first conversation, Justina told him that she was the daughter of a liaison between a Dutch military officer and a Sundanese woman. Though her parents had never formally married and her father had long since returned to the Netherlands, Justina liked to use her father's Dutch family name of Oostenbroek. Once she knew Van Es well, she would often tease him:

"Your name is too simple. If we were married we could use a combination of both. Van Es-Oostenbroek! That sounds much grander. Or perhaps just Van Oostenbroek! With a name like that you'd be sure to be promoted!"

Justina spoke enough Dutch to be able to hold a passable conversation and this fact alone commended her doubly to Van Es. Many of the Inlander women could speak only a few words of Dutch and, naturally, had no education. While their bodies alone may have been enough for the rank and file, a man like Van Es was doubly pleased if he could talk with his love. Justina not only spoke fluent Dutch but possessed something of the ability typical of Europeans to think laterally, to anticipate events and to remember things. Since she could understand him and his world yet was completely outside the military, Van Es felt he could safely unburden himself to her.

When he saw her first, he was at Atek's, sitting in a cubicle, facing the curtained entrance, with his arm around the waist of another girl. As Justina came through the curtain, her beauty was luminous in the flickering light of the gas lamps. More important, she seemed to enter and look directly at Van Es. Momentarily, the Major returned what he assumed was her forthright look. She sat at a table opposite to him with some other girls and looked across at him continually. When his little playmate, Siti, left him for a few minutes, Van Es smiled treacherously at Justina and raised his glass. She smiled back in a way which suggested either that he should prefer her to Siti or that she knew that he already did so. Siti returned and sat on his right in such a position that he could continue to flirt with Justina over her shoulder. Justina left no doubt that she was his if he wanted her. Van Es pretended that he needed to relieve himself and on his return sent Siti to buy more drinks at the other end of the crowded room. Sauntering casually up to Justina's table he told her in Dutch that he had not seen her before and asked if she would come again. Justina smiled winsomely up at him and said simply:

"Tomorrow."

"I will look for you here tomorrow," Van Es said, with a smile he hoped was 'bewitching'.

Siti came back and, as she sat down, Justina smiled knowingly over her shoulder into his eyes, as if to say: "Now I know you prefer me."

Van Es headed home early and he would have been surprised to see Justina immediately fill his vacant seat.

"He didn't want you tonight?" Justina asked matter-of-factly, offering her friend a hand-rolled cigarette.

"I think it's you he wants," replied Siti, blowing a smoke ring with great nonchalance. "He kept looking at you whenever he could."

"You noticed!"

"Of course, but no problem. We are friends."

Justina smiled and rose to her feet, smoothing down her ankle-length dress in the process.

"I'm going home. too."

Next day, Van Es found it impossible to concentrate properly. Usually, he didn't think much about the girls he met. But there was something about Justina that infatuated him. The whole day, her face haunted him, her dark, liquid, eyes gazed promisingly into his. He found himself snapping at local soldiers who were late, or who had forgotten something, or who made mistakes.

"Is this the way you were taught," he exploded continually, his fair face red with angry frustration. "When will you ever learn discipline! How can we expect to achieve anything if we have to all the time work in this constant muddle. Just follow the procedures. Get it right, do it right," he barked again and again.

His afternoon siesta was ruined because Justina's image refused to leave his mind! Drinks and dinner at the mess were amiable enough but he checked and re-checked the time with the great, black and white, wooden clock behind the bar.

"Van Es, for God's sake cut it out," an irritated officer eventually blurted out good-naturedly.

Van Es gave a slight smile. "What?"

"Looking at the God-damn clock every few minutes. That's what."

It was the end of the month. Everyone was in a good mood. Everyone had money.

The officer gripped him tightly by the shoulder, leaning over him.

"I suppose you can't wait to be off to the pasar malam (night market) for a woman!"

Van Es smiled more broadly and tossed his head back to drain his glass before shouting for more beer.

"Let's all go and look at Van Es's woman," teased his friend, leering around the circle. We know where you go. You always go to the same place."

There was nothing for it. When the time came, instead of arriving at Pak Atek's alone for a romantic rendezvous, Van Es had half-a-dozen boozed-up colleagues in tow. By the time they arrived the only thing on their minds was more drink and women of their own. Van Es realised immediately that Justina was there but she kept away from his group after catching his eye to signal that she knew he had seen her. The group was well on its way to getting roaring drunk but, while appearing to be one of the gang, Van Es drank more slowly until he caught Justina's eye again and nodded at the door. She had remained all the time ostensibly engrossed with a gaggle of girl friends but, like him, she had one eye on them and one eye on him. She saw his signal and waited for him to go out of the back of the building to where the lavatories were. Van Es walked round the side of the hut, through the bamboos, and met her at the front. Although they had hardly even spoken, there was already a bond between them which needed no articulation.

"Let's go to Karim's," he told her, walking away briskly.

It was difficult for her to hurry in her long, European skirt and heeled boots but she tried her best to keep up with the strides of his tall figure, sometimes almost running beside him. Pak Karim's was only about a hundred metres further along the same road and round to the right so it wasn't worth taking a carriage if the weather was dry. Karim's was virtually identical with Atek's but more popular with other ranks than with officers. When they entered the crowded room, some men made way for them and, after ordering drinks, Van Es sat down beside her, with his arm already round her shoulders. It was the first time that they had touched and Van Es found himself instantly overpowered by her delectable perfume, like a dog after a scent. He nuzzled her head gently merely to be able to breath in more of the seductive aroma.

"You like my perfume," Justina giggled.

"I could follow it to the end of the earth," said Van Es.

Justina smiled again and nuzzled him back.

"Are you living in barracks?" she asked.

"Close by," he said with an officer's caution.

A waiter in a sarong brought him a beer and her a young coconut from which to drink the milk and spoon the tender white flesh.

"Are you married?" she asked, looking at him sideways through her long lashes.

"If I was married I wouldn't be here," Van Es joked.

Justina squeezed his knee with her hand, under the table. Van Es rubbed her back and held her close, drugged by her closeness and the irresistible power of her perfume.

All too frequently, conversations with girls, at places like this, often went very little but because Justina could speak Dutch fluently and could understand him, she was almost like a European date, except that her appearance gave her the exotic mystery of the East. After only a few minutes they were talking and laughing quite naturally together like old friends. Van Es was genuinely interested in her and since nothing succeeds like interest or flattery Justina told him openly and honestly about her family, where she lived and what she did. She had looked rather quiet when Van Es first saw her but, tonight she chattered animatedly, leaving him little time to talk about himself, even had he wanted to - which he did not. It was clear that Justina liked him and the more he felt her soft curves through the thin stuff of her clothes and felt her close to him, the more Van Es liked her. She was fun, she was soft, she was enchanting.

Justina could easily sense his attraction.

"Shall we go home together?" she asked, laying her head on his shoulder.

Van Es's body ached to take her but he never took women to the villa until he was quite sure that he could manage them, most importantly, that they would leave quietly when told. Those he did take home to the villa he always insisted went home before daylight. Otherwise, it would show things to others that he would rather they did not see and give him a reputation that perhaps, in some quarters, would do him no good. Atek had some dingy rooms at the back and whenever he was tempted he would take a girl there. It wasn't pleasant because the bamboo walls were paper thin and each couple could hear the shouts, the laughter, the curses and finally the grunts and groans of others getting as far into each other as they possibly could.

"We can go to Atek's," said Van Es. "He has

rooms there."

Justina pouted. "Not Atek's", she pleaded. "I want to go to your house with you."

Van Es tried as hard as he could to persuade her but she told him what he already knew - that Atek's place was dirty and stinking - inferring that it was no place for two lovers, especially two lovers who were virtually both Europeans.

"No, not Atek's," she repeated. "Your house." Let's go to your house."

The more Van Es refused to take her home with him the more Justina exited him with her hugs and kisses. But security was security. No woman was worth jeopardising his career. In the end, Justina could no more move Van Es than he could move her. He wanted her because she had aroused the desperate lust of a bachelor soldier. She wanted him because she saw prospects?

That night, it was much tougher for Van Es to turn his back on Justina than it was for her to say good night to him. Van Es reeled off home in an agony of burning desire which kept him awake for hours. Justina went back to Pak Atek's and chatted easily to her friends before she, too, went home through the deserted streets.

Taking part in the service in Willemskerk next morning, it was no understatement to say that Van Es felt less than well. Even the short walk from his villa to the great, domed, church had failed to kick-start him. It had been a very late and sleepless night followed by the usual very early Sunday morning. And, immediately he had opened his eyes, he could think only of Justina. Perhaps he should have brought her home, after all. What a different night he would have had then! Knowing how easy it would have been to have had her tortured him all the more. Then again, suppose she had proved difficult and wanted to linger at his place? He could not have missed Sunday church but what could he have done with her if she refused to go home?

Van Es stood up and sat down in his chair automatically whenever prayers were said or hymns sung. He was usually a strong singer but this day his lips merely formed the words. Each time the organ began to play, with a veritable broadside of nerve-jarring sound, Van Es's heart literally missed a beat. Under-the-weather though he was, he was alert enough to think how much he disliked hearing the Minister sermonise about the need to be fair to the natives! Their place was simply to obey and follow; everybody knew that. And what a struggle it was to get them to do it! Even when you gave them every regulation and procedure known to man they would still find some circumvention or other - or just ignore them. Van Es clenched his jaw tightly. It was discipline and order these people needed, not fairness. If you gave them fairness they'd do whatever they liked!

"Maybe that's their secret plan," he liked to joke. 'If they can't kick us out on the battlefield, perhaps they think they can drive us crazy with all their weird ways."

Van Es was glad when the black bibles and brown hymn- books were put away and he could join the others filing slowly out of the cavernous, domed and pillared building. Normally, he always enjoyed Sunday church because Willemskerk made him feel somehow closer to his home in The Netherlands than to the vastly different tropical world beyond the bright, white, walls with their huge windows and immensely tall and narrow European doors. It had been cool in the church and, once outside, he felt revived by the warmth of the early morning sun. The day was young and there was still a mood of everything just starting up. Van Es decided to walk by himself, under the trees, around the perimeter of Koningsplein.

First, it was necessary to cross the railway line and pass through Gambir, the area which by mid-afternoon would already shaping up to become the pasar malam or night market. Beyond Gambir, the bare grass of Koningsplein stretched like a vast, green 'desert'. Everyone who visited Batavia commented on it. Some said it was large enough to build a second city. Others said that its vast, open, spaces made them feel vulnerable. Others marvelled at its majesty at the heart of the capital city of the Netherlands Indies. Even its name, King's Plain, was majestic.

And how symptomatic of the scale of intended Dutch endeavours in the Indies to be able to create a plain of such immense size. Around it were government offices, military headquarters, the villas of the highest ranking officials and the palace of the Governor General - all immense and spacious in keeping with the size of the plain.

To the natives it was just a hot, dusty, wasted bit of land. To Dutchmen it was a symbol of imperial greatness, the great, gleaming, white buildings around its perimeter were symbols of imperial greatness. On special days, such as the Queen's Birthday, the military, living symbols of this imperial greatness, could fill even this enormous field with their cavalry, infantry and artillery parading magnificently beneath the waving flags of their regiments.

Van Es loved those parades. It made him proud to be a Dutchman!

The sheer grandeur of Koningsplein somehow made Van Es feel imperial and heroic! He was in uniform, and, as he walked, local people kept well out of his way. Having any kind of misunderstanding or, worse, an altercation, with a man in uniform could be very bad news indeed. Inlanders found blue eyes chilling and the fact that Van Es's eyes could hardly be seen beneath the peak of his helmet tended to sew even more fear. There were no merry greetings or waves. But then he didn't expect it. Discipline was what was needed in the Indies and to have discipline one must have respect not presumptuous, disorderly, greetings from every scrawny native who passed. It was now the height of the day and very hot so Van Es abandoned his plan to walk all the way home. He was fit, but, by the time he reached the villa, he'd be sweating like a pig. There were always carriages hanging about under the trees hoping for customers and he swung up into a sado.

The pony clattered forward at a flick from the driver's whip, a bright red ball of cotton bouncing decoratively on top of the horse's head. Tiny bells hung from its harness and jingled as the carriage sped along the dusty roads. The breeze was refreshing under the carriage's awning and the flapping of long, narrow, flags at each side of the driver increased the feeling of being in the midst of cool winds. Van Es liked riding in sados. They were easy to get into and he could sprawl comfortably in the back with his long legs stretched out. The delman and bigger carriages could carry more passengers but Van Es always felt that sitting sideways, as one had to do in a delman, was not at all comfortable. And it was difficult to get in and out. As they drove, a sense of anti-climax grew in him. At the end of the walk he had felt vigorous and strong again. But it was Sunday and he hated Sundays because they seemed even quieter than he imagined the grave could be. He had nothing to do and by the time the sado had reached his district he was already winding down.

The tropics was not a place for vigour. There seemed always to be a lot of doing nothing and waiting, of lying idle on one's bed in the intolerable heat of mid-day, waiting for the sun to set. If there was really little else to do on Sunday afternoon except sleep, the tradition of rysttafel (rice table) for Sunday lunch virtually guaranteed this would be all that happened.

The Officer's Mess had a very good rysttafel and it didn't take much to persuade Van Es that he would have nothing to do by himself at the villa and that he would be far better off guaranteeing that he slept all afternoon by partaKing of the mess's famed rice table.

A long table had been set up at one end of the mess covered by a white table cloth. Rysttafel was particularly suitable for a buffet and for feeding large numbers of people. A rysttafel was never only one dish. It was rarely less than ten. Often it was fifteen or more dishes of every conceivable content, mixture and ingredient - meats, fish, vegetables, curries, sauces, spices, rice and plenty of assorted fruit to follow. Rysttafel was not for the squeamish or for the sensitive stomach, but, once you got used to its distinctive tastes and flavours, it was a feast to be looked forward to. The officers had it only on Sundays, when they had time to do it justice, but guests at hotels could expect it every day. After lunch, when they all felt suitably bloated, when spice and chillis had made their throats and tongues as hot as fire and with sweat pouring down their collars from puce faces, the guests would retire to their rooms, throw off their tight clothes and sleep until close to sunset. Then you would see them, dressed like strange looKing Inlanders, men and women alike, in sarongs and flip-flops, sitting outside their rooms arranged around little open gardens, enjoying tea and the cool of the late afternoon.

Van Es's afternoon was not dissimilar. When he woke from his siesta he, too, wrapped a comfortable sarong round his waist and sat out on the front veranda in a comfortable rattan chair while Sup served him Indies coffee and he smoked a fat Deli cigar. The sound of Indies music wafted to him, here and there a street vendor cried the name of his wares or rang a tinkling bell to announce his arrival.

While he sat and smoked, he thought again of Justina. It wasn't his custom to go out on a Sunday evening, except to the mess or the Club. On Monday, duty called, bright and early. And Van Es was far from being a man who did not take duty seriously. What man thirsting for promotion could? But, recently, his nights at the mess and the Club had begun to be as boring as his work. The sheer repetition was boring! And unless he went home more or less drunk, which he often did, the nights were lonely. It was very beautiful in the early evening, peaceful, relaxed, the sun casting long shadows, the servants spraying water to keep down the dust of the day or watering plants. Here and there a trickle of smoke marked the spot where weeds or household garbage was being burnt. The late afternoon seemed somehow a endless and yet it disappeared faster than any other part of the day except dawn. Dawn crept up on one but was nowhere near as enjoyable as a lingering afternoon, when the world winds down and the tasks are done.

Already in his mind's eye he could see Atek's hut with its woven bamboo walls in its bamboo grove filled with twinkling lights. Already he could hear the tinkling laughter of the girls. Already the tropical sickness of the night had him in its grip. Already he could taste what he had tantalisingly tasted last night - the cool, silky, wine sweet lips of Justina!

He told himself that he must not go to Atek's. He was very busy tomorrow. He was always very busy on Mondays. Yet he would like to see her. Just seeing her didn't necessarily mean a late night, didn't necessarily mean sleeping with her. But if he was close to her he would want to sleep with her! He didn't know which was worse; being driven crazy not seeing her or being driven crazy by seeing her but not having her! For sure she would not agree to go to a back room with him. Anyway, he himself hadn't time for all that tonight. Certainly, there could be no question of bringing her back to the villa because he had only met her once and first impressions can be dangerously superficial. He would need to know a lot more about her before he could bring her home. But he knew all this and he was a strong and resolute man who rarely wavered. He was certain that he could see her, have fun with her and say "good night" to her. He could!

But would she be there at all? Maybe, after last night, she had given up on him? After all, it was clients she was looKing for, not boyfriends. Maybe, after he left, she had giggled and hugged with some other man! He had never seen her at Atek's before and it would be a miracle if she turned up there two nights in a row. But, suppose she did? And he wasn't there! Would she look for him? Was she interested in him? If he went, would he find her kissing another man? Would it matter? Yes, it would matter! There was something about Justina that he liked. He knew her trade, yet she had spoken to him forthrightly like a friend, and a friend like her was what Van Es craved - not a wife, not a proper girlfriend but someone whom he could regard as a friend when he chose and who could be available when he chose - and not available when he didn't. Justina fitted his notions of order very well. There was also something about her that made him resent the thought of her with another man. In fact, if she had not been a 'lady of the night' Van Es could easily imagine that he was falling in love with her, such was thc spell she had cast over him.

It was no use. He had to try to see her again. He decided that, after a very few drinks and a very light supper at the mess, he would make his way to Atek's, satisfy his craving, and return home, alone and early.

When the sado dropped him off outside Atek's,

for some reason, he felt nervous and his pulse was actually high. "I must really care about this girl," he told himself, adding vehemently 'but that's completely asinine!" Atek himself, with a couple of henchman, was squatting down close to the front door, passing the time, shooting the breeze and all smoking contentedly.

"Selamat malam, Tuan," ("Good evening, Sir") Atek said nodding to him with a knowing smile.

"Selamat malam Atek," returned Van Es, neither warmly nor coldly, but as brusquely as he felt a high military official should speak to a native - even one with whom he had a passing acquaintance.

"Banyak wanita ini malam," smiled Atek obsequiously. "Mari, Tuan, masuk, masuk. (Many girls tonight. Please go inside.")

Van Es was no sooner inside than he felt rather than saw Justina bound happily towards him and throw her arms round his neck. Even though a man with a soldier's strength, she almost pulled him off balance with her exuberance. His heart stopped racing. She was there! She was waiting for him! Unquestionably, she liked him! She led him to a rickety table in a dark corner, drinks were served, they lit cigarettes and chatted together in Dutch.

"I thought perhaps you would not come," she said, laughing and nestling close to him like a genuinely lovesick girl.

"I thought that perhaps you would not come," said Van Es.

Van Es's arm went quickly round her and, as before, they talked and laughed and petted in the dark corner. Atek's was nearly empty but, as the owner had promised, there were quite a few girls but only about half-a-dozen, mainly young and mainly junior, officers. It was hard for soldiers living in barracks. Young bureaucrats, merchants or planters would sooner rather than later acquire a housekeeper but soldiers had nowhere to put her, except the barracks. For them, girls at places like Atek's seemed a viable option - especially since they could be changed, without obligation, as often as one liked. For a young man it was paradise indeed!

Van Es was a little older than most of those around him and, while it was true that he didn't want the responsibility of a proper wife or even of a housekeeper, he was getting bored with a succession of different women who could give him nothing except sex. Hence, the instant electricity in his 'relationship' with Justina. Van Es was no bookworm, no lover of the arts. He was not one of those who hungered for the culture of the Netherlands while grubbing for money in the Indies. But he was an officer with an officer's background. He needed a woman and he also welcomed the companionship of a woman. This was the special promise of Justina.

Van Es always thought it incredible how quickly one could become intimate with an Indies woman. Not that Justina was a full Indies girl. It was not only that she was not black, but aspects of her culture and even her nature had been influenced by her white blood. Thankfully, the one element that was not different was her easy sensuality. While Van Es loved rules and procedures with which to do his job, how he hated the formality and stiffness of the European 'courtship'. How many times had he proved that an hour's courtship of an Indies woman was enough! Justina's skin was soft and cool, like all Inlander women, but almost Chinese in its porcelain colouring. And she had that tiger wildness of all Indies women, as if she had just come, untamed, from the jungle. Her willingness, her wildness and her doll like beauty, set off by the mysterious, almost sinister, black of her eyes and hair, mesmerised Van Es. He had to have her!

But, there was no possibility of taking her to the villa tonight. Weekdays were busy for Van Es and his programme was especially heavy next week so he knew that he could not even see her again until at least Wednesday. But then Thursday was a worKing day, too, and it would be unthinkable to take her home. And Friday was the Queen's Birthday so the earliest that they could meet would be next Saturday!

This time, their parting was even more frustrating for Van Es than the first. Not a night, but a whole week, separated them. She clung to him when they got up to leave. Atek and his men appeared to be nowhere around and, when they parted, each kissed the other passionately in the dark privacy of the bamboo grove. From behind some giant clumps, their dark faces almost invisible between the leaves, Atek and his men looked on silently. Van Es virtually had to tear himself away, jump into a sado and head for home. He dare not look back in case she was still standing there, watching wistfully his departing carriage. But Justina did not linger. She was a practical girl. He had given her a few coins tonight and she, too, moved to board a sado.

"Selamat Malam, Atek," she seemed to say to the dark bamboos as she turned to leave. She heard a faint rustling of grass or leaves. Atek and his bouncers were squatting on the ground, in the dark, behind the bamboos, but there was no reply. As the owner of the establishment, Atek expected cheap girls like Justina to address him respectfully as 'Pak Atek'. It offended and irritated him that she always addressed him as "Atek", putting herself on a level with the Dutch. Often she placed a special stress on "Atek" as if to infer that his name dirtied her mouth.

It would be an understatement to say that Justina and Atek did not get on. Atek was always asKing her for money, as if it was his right to have it because she patronised his place - a kind of unofficial rent. Many of the girls were employed by him and gave him all their earnings. But not Justina. As far as she was concerned, she was just a customer. Atek did not own her and she owed him nothing. Justina resented deeply his constant requests and Atek in turn was deeply upset by her responses. She was using his place and, as a result, made money, so it was only fair to share some of her good fortune with him.

"If I didn't come here, I could go somewhere else," Justina would retort angrily and imperiously, whenever he asked. "I don't have to pay you just because I might meet a friend on your premises."

"The other girls pay."

"That's because they're frightened of you."

Then Justina would lecture him about the difference between Indies ways of doing business and the ways of the belanda (the Dutch).

"Business is business," she would scold him. "If I buy something from you, I will pay for it. If I don't you should not always be expecting money as a gift. Everything should be straight and above board.."

"It's our tradition to help one another," Atek would mock-plead, all the time hating her the more.

"I don't care," Justina would fume. "It's an Inlander tradition and it's backward!"

Traditionally, island people were endlessly curious about what everyone else was doing, but Justina also felt that Atek poked his nose where it didn't belong - for example, apparently spying on her clandestinely from behind the bushes. Atek would have said that he was there accidentally. Justina would have said that he was there on purpose and then the two would argue, Justina, haughty and imperious, and as voluble as only a woman can be, and Atek silent with resentment, after maKing his point tersely and without much expression in his lined face.

Justina flurried out of the garden, settled into the back of a sado, and disappeared into the night.

"Dutch bitch!" muttered Atek to his men.

"Only thinks she's Dutch, Pak," said one of the men sarcastically, "but a bitch all right!"

"Yeah, yeah, yeah" said Atek. Her mother's a pure Sundanese from Bandung so she's just a native like the rest of us!"

There was smothered laughter behind the bushes and the sound of vigorous spitting.

On Tuesday, Van Es had to renew a supply contract so he spent a chunk of Monday, not only checKing the market prices but taKing advice about trends. It was part of his job to keep abreast of such matters but, on the eve of a contract signing, ambient knowledge had to be sharpened to definite, up-to-date, facts. When, next day, the Chinese merchant quoted his price, Van Es scoffed loudly and flung down his pencil on the desk.

"Outrageous, my friend. Outrageous."

He named a much lower price.

"This is what the price should be."

The Chinaman smiled.

"Too low, Tuan. Cannot," he said amicably, resenting Van Es's detailed knowledge of the market. It was always preferable to do business when people could be confused or hoodwinked either through inadequate information or too much. But Van Es was clever. he studied everything, knew everything. Very hard to increase a margin with him.

Negotiating prices in the Indies was a game. The seller always set them artificially high but the buyer always bid artificially low until, after bidding and counter bidding, a satisfactory compromise was reached.

"I hope you're not trying to rob me," said Van Es.

"We are not trying to rob you Tuan," the Chinaman replied plaintively, secretly well aware that he would if he could get away with it. "But we must make a little profit or how are we to live?"

"I'm sure you have a huge mansion tucked away somewhere," Van Es laughed sceptically.

"Oh, no. My home is very humble, Tuan," said the Chinaman, using a stock phrase. "Maybe one day you want to come and see for yourself?" he said, knowing full well that Van Es never would.

The Chinaman protested, Van Es was adamant.

"Take it or leave it," Van Es said arrogantly. "There are plenty of other suppliers."

"You are very hard," Tuan, the Chinaman said, but accepted the price offered because, even so, the profit was actually enough. Still, if he could have got more.........

"You cannot squeeze much out of a Dutchman," he said to his companion as they walked out of the compound to one of Batavia's very few limousines, parked under a tree and surrounded by an army of ragged but curious onlookers. Only the Governor General had one comparable. "Stingy, stingy, people."

It was the end of the month so this was also the week when Van Es had to do his book keeping. The staff hated these times because all day long, day after day, Van Es would be calling for files, checKing and re-checking figures, finding mistakes, trying to force down expenses.

"Why have we spent so much on this", he would demand. "Do we have to pay for that. Couldn't we have got it for free by doing it ourselves."

Before the week was over he would have gone through the unit's expenditure with a fine tooth comb, ensuring that every guilder was accounted for and prudently spent. Not a few contractors went away with the message that they must recalculate their charges before Van Es would pay.

"Nobody can pull the wool over my eyes," was

his constant boast.

Van Es enjoyed this part of his job. He knew that his prudence was worthwhile and appreciated by his superiors. He felt himself to be in the very front line of defence of the Netherlands Indies Government's always slender budgetary resources. After all, overspending was as serious an enemy as the flesh and blood ones on the battlefield. And it kept him extremely busy at a time when, in quieter moments, his mind might have wandered to Justina. The day's were hectic and after drinks and dinner at the mess every night he was quite ready for bed.

At the end of the week it was the Queen's Birthday celebrated by balls and parties throughout the Netherlands Indies. The Governor General's Ball was naturally the largest and most prestigious and, as a senior officer, Van Es was privileged to receive an invitation.

The whole day of the Queen's Birthday was a public holiday. Early in the morning even the vast open expanse of Koningsplein was filled by the Netherlands Indies security forces. Van Es was also on parade. Besides European troops and officers, there were men from Sulawesi, from Ambon and the Malukus and, of course, from Java. The Europeans were by no means a homogenous group. Although mainly Dutch, the officers included Germans, French and Scandanavians. Van Es always found it particularly moving to watch a good military parade. But it was no fun taKing part. The sun was hot, whatever the time of day, a lot of time was spent standing waiting a turn to parade, there were long speeches to listen to and, after a while, the uniforms that looked so impressive from a distance, became extremely uncomfortable. Local Indies leaders were invited to sit on a shaded dais with the Governor General while he took the salute. There could be no greater demonstration of raw Dutch power in the Indies than a military parade like this - the rows and rows of infantry, European cavalry with pennants flying, horse-drawn artillery, the elite palace guard, marines, police, special anti-guerrilla units, logistics and supply corps and band after military band, each playing more stirring and moving music than the last. As a spectator, it made Van Es shiver with pride.

Watching natives shared none of these emotions, but any who happened to be around usually looked on curiously. One could not say that in this situation that they were afraid, but recent defeats of Indies forces in Aceh and Bali after a long succession of 19th Century wars. practically throughout the archipelago, including Java, had certainly taught them to respect the tenacity if not the power of the colonial army.

But, among the Indies leaders, it was a tempered by the suppressed but ever-present desire to be lords of their own lands once again. If the leader's respect was forced, they nevertheless took good care, while ostensibly worKing hand in glove with their foreign masters, to squeeze them for as much as they could get. For their part, the Dutch were grateful that, instead of continuous, unsettling and expensive fighting, some of the Indies leaders could be 'bought' in this way. And, on days like this, there was a deep residual sense that those who would not be bought could be crushed, of the inexorable expansion and consolidation of Dutch military power and control over the Indies.

The Queen's Birthday Ball was held in the evening of the same day. At the best of times, the Governor's glittering, white, palace looked like something out of the Arabian Nights. But, at night, illuminated by thousands of gas and kerosene lights, with flags flying and ceremonial guards standing stiffly to attention everywhere, the palace became the epitome of an idyllic Dutch view of the Indies as islands of limitless wealth.

Few noticed or wanted to notice the dusky faces of the true, bare-foot, indigenous owners of this land, loitering curiously behind the perimeter railings and hedges, their great, dark eyes, watching their white overlords wallow in pageantry and riches. Throughout the Dutch Indies, the whites were like shining stars occupying centre stage, perpetually surrounded by shadowy brown 'helpers' whom they took so much for granted that, as they ran to answer their every beck and call, they had long ago ceased even to see them.

At the top of the long, wide steps leading into the palace, beneath the sparkling chandeliers, through the massive, white, mock 'Grecian' pillars, one entered rooms of unparalleled sumptuousness. Greco/Roman statues stood in every niche in the wall, lamps glittered everywhere, footsteps were muffled by thick, ornately patterned carpets, heavy, crimson, velvet curtains were drawn back to each side of the great windows and held in place by gold tassels, huge pictures of military figures and former governor generals hung in heavy, gilt, frames around the walls.

A long line of carriages queued to enter the driveway and an even longer queue of people filed slowly along a receiving line to be greeted by the Governor General himself and his lady. The Governor General was in full ceremonial uniform, complete with sashes and medals. His lady was resplendent in a light blue gown, topped off with a sparkling diamond Sitira.

The Queen's Birthday Ball brought together all sections of the Netherlands Indies community which mattered - including important local leaders, especially the inland sultans. The rich, apparently highly eclectic dress of the Indies leaders, contrasted with the more conservative-looking, formal apparel of the Europeans. The male Indies nobility either wore Javanese or Sundanese hats, embroidered velvet tunics with gold buttons, a wide sash with a bejewelled kris and intricately patterned sarongs. Their ladies, slim in figure-hugging, floral, sheaths, tottered on heeled slippers, gold ornaments vibrating in their hair as they moved, and, each one in a brightly coloured and ornately embroidered kebaya or blouse. The Indies leaders and their copious numbers of retainers found themselves in the midst of an intimidating crowd of senior bureaucrats from the all important civil administration, military personnel and private merchants and plantation operators. (Not so many of the latter because the Indies' rougher diamonds rarely came to Batavia for anything, let alone balls.) To be forced to mingle with so many Dutch people was always an overpowering and taxing experience. But, understanding the stress they came under and obviously wishing to make the Indies leaders feel welcome, they were never left to their own devises but, as befitted their station, they were given constant 'brotherly' attention by the most senior officials and were never allowed to be far from the Governor General himself.

Van Es, too, was in full ceremonial uniform, black broad cloth from head to foot with glinting, embossed, silver buttons, silver braid over his left shoulder, his left hand on his sword hilt, his helmet under his right arm. He and each of his fellow officers snapped to attention when it was their turn to be greeted by the Governor General, shook hands with the Lady Governor and, after depositing swords and helmets at the cloak room, filed slowly into the ballroom where drinks on silver trays were being carried round by an army of white-tuniced waiters in sarongs. There was food, buffet style, in rooms leading from left and right off the huge ballroom and guests drank, chatted and ate while they waited for the formal proceedings to begin. The most important of these was the speech and loyal toast by the Governor General. And then the Governor General and his lady took to the dance floor giving the signal that others may do so also. The military band struck up a lively number and the colourful couples began to twirl around.

The room was packed with the black evening suits of the bureaucrats and private businessmen, the brilliant uniforms of officers of every branch of the service and the butterfly-bright dresses of ladies who turned out en masse for the occasion, wearing their finest jewellery. Finally, there were the exotic costumes of the Indies leaders and their retinues, the floral, batik dresses of the ladies reflecting the fabulous colour of the Indies countryside.

Watching with his group regular of cronies, Van Es was struck by how many more white women there were at the Ball than in previous years. Of course, this was not the Concordia Club, where men always dominated, and many were the wives and daughters of bureaucrats or private businessmen, but there seemed to be more than ever of unattached European females brought along as friends or relations. While he enjoyed seeing them, and while he enjoyed dancing, dancing in this company had its dangers. He was always afraid to show interest in the very few Dutch belles who were usually available in Batavia because he was certain that after one dance the girl, or, worse still, the girl's mother, would expect him to call, and a relationship to develop, and this was something he didn't want to be bothered with. He had his own sources of girls who gave him no trouble at all!

Van Es was content to circulate with a drink in one hand, chatting amiably, maKing new acquaintances and renewing old ones - usually among fellow officers, exchanging views and news - especially about who had been promoted recently or, more importantly who might be. The Ball was an occasion of high protocol and no junior officer could speak to a senior without being addressed first. Like everyone else, Van Es found himself stressed by the need to be constantly alert and to be always doing and saying the right things at the right time to the right people. Nevertheless, occasions like this were hot-beds of intriguing speculation about changes in the service and, naturally, of gossip about scandals and disgrace. Husbands with wives had the opportunity to be plugged into a second network and, later, at home, their wives would relay all the juicy bits of gossip, scandal and plain intelligence they had gleaned from other men's wives in the most enjoyable possible orgy of exchanges. From a colonial wife's point of view, who wanted to dance when one could gossip instead!

Van Es was wished a good evening by Meneer Hogendorp, Colonel of his regiment.

"Good to see you Van Es. You're doing a great job," the Colonel smiled sociably.

"Thank you, Sir."

"I've been wanting to talk to you about your future but we're all a bit busy at the moment."

"Sir!"

"I'll get my adjutant to set up an appointment for you during the next few weeks. How's the stock-taKing going along?"

Van Es briefed him generally about the achievements and challenges of the commissary before the Colonel took the initiative to move on.

"Something's in the wind," one of his close friends, Major de Korte, told him jokingly.

"I just hope it's not the Ordnance Corps," Van Es joked back.

The Queen's Birthday Ball always left Van Es with a deep sense of living the good life. Luxurious surroundings, elegant company of the highest official and social standing, association, however formal and distant, with the people at the 'top', an indelible sense of privilege and of command. The Queen's Birthday with all of its formality, glamour and the kudos attaching to those attending it was a celebration of Dutch rule. Van Es exhaled smoke from his cigar with deep satisfaction. The Ball was the rulers' night. This was how he had imagined the Indies. This was the life for which he had come to the Indies.

But how to get closer to the 'top' than the Commissary? How to do more apparently important things than arrange basic supplies?

Toward the end of the evening, as carriages began to leave, there was an enormous fireworks display on the wide, front lawn of the palace, so that the guests clattered away beneath kaleidoscopic sprays of fire.

Van Es went straight home. Just for a moment, Atek's dingy hut flashed into his mind, but the sheer weight of the magnificence of this special evening banished it just as quickly. Before going to sleep, he sat for a long time in an easy chair on his veranda, a great orange moon shedding a faint light over the garden, still wearing full ceremonial uniform, to prolong the deeply enjoyable feeling he had of pride, of power, of Dutch rule over the bounteous garden of the Indies. Eventually, the trappings of position and power had to be taken off and put away and, as usual, he slept in a sarong beneath a mosquito net.

The next day was Saturday, and Van Es awoke rather late and feeling somewhat exhausted by the events of the past week. Sup brought him morning coffee on the veranda and the usual breakfast of coffee, toast, eggs and fruit. He usually played soccer on a Saturday morning but it was much too late for that now; he needed to be out by six o'clock in the morning if he wanted to join the game. He guessed that the teams might be sadly depleted on this morning after the night before. But it was expected and nobody minded as long as absence didn't occur too often. As with everything he did, Van Es was a serious player, but everyone understood that mornings like this were special.

Instead, he decided to go to the European shopping centre, opposite the Harmonie Club, in an area known as Ryswyk. He needed new casual shoes and they would stock European sizes there. Like most men, especially soldiers, he was not a shopper by nature, but apart from the fact that new shoes were essential, sometimes he enjoyed the European ambience of the place. True, in places, there were plenty of traditional Chinese shophouses, but there were also many buildings the architecture of which had been lifted straight from Holland - especially the distinctive roofs, dormer windows and shutters.

The shops at Harmonie, like those at nearby Pasar Baru, were a mixture of Dutch and Chinese - at Harmonie, majority were Dutch, at Pasar Baru, majority of the shops were owned and run by Chinese. Inlanders performed all the menial services inside and outside, such as fetching an order from the stock room, opening and closing doors, running errands, flagging down transport, keeping the shop and the area outside clean, putting out and taking in the sun blinds. The owners of these premises went to extraordinary lengths to make the appearance of their shops as European as possible and to ship in not only staples but the very latest fashions from Holland and elsewhere in which they guessed and hoped their clients would be interested. Trade always needs change so 'new arrivals' were the lifeblood of these retail outlets.

The first motor vehicles had arrived in Batavia a few years previously. At first the city government had expressed great concern about the dangers to pedestrians posed by these fast and noisy vehicles and the threat to the surface of the roads. Natives who had never seen a motor vehicle were always very frightened. They were so big, so powerful and aggressive, so fast, so unpredictable and, if one hit you, so lethal. Of course, they had long known about steam trains and trams and a ride through the city was always very popular with those who could afford it. There was usually a concentration of motor vehicles in the business area, close to Kali Besar, and in the up-market shopping areas of Harmonie and Pasar Baru. But, still, there were not many, because they were expensive even for the rich.

Van Es felt good about seeing the very latest technology on the streets of Batavia. Many a time he had congratulated himself on the good fortune of being allowed to live in the opening years of the 20th Century. Change was everywhere in the air and everywhere everything was speeding up. Trains, trams, motor cars - the common denominator was the machine! They were now living in the machine age, an age which was destined to speed up life beyond any man's current hopes or fears. Man was on the brink of incredible new destinies, thanks to the machine. Machines were making possible new things, for example, great ships like the Titanic! Everywhere more was being achieved, faster than ever before. People walked faster, worked faster. Even the new music was fast! To be alive was to feel swept up in a rush of progress. Progress that could be seen visibly around Batavia and Java. Everywhere, great new buildings were going up, offices, barracks, factories and shops with a distinctive Indies architecture which was even the envy of Holland!

In the new Batavia, with its many new shops with dazzling window displays filled with the latest goods and gadgetry from Europe, it felt good to be able to shop as if one was at home in Holland. In fact, some people were even suggesting that kampong Belanda or Dutch villages should be developed so that the growing numbers of Dutch people arriving from the Netherlands could live more or less as they did at home - plus servants.

Saturday was a time for shopping and the pavements were quite crowded, mainly with Europeans, seemingly all dressed in tropical whites, from the long dresses of the ladies to the boaters and solar topees of the men. Natives loitered everywhere, waiting to serve their European masters, and, here and there, one might see an Indies woman with a child bouncing in a selandang (sling) on her hip, or a Chinese madame protecting her fair skin with a sun shade. Batavia had always been a cosmopolitan town and, in the commercial districts, it was common to see side by side, turbaned Indians and

Arabs, pigtailed Chinaman and colourfully dressed islanders from as far away as Sulawesi and Ambon in the East or the batak lands of north Sumatra.

Dressed in spotless white and going in and our of their spotless white buildings the Europeans looked like gods in some earthly heaven who had inexplicable become mixed up with the ubiquitous, ragged-looKing, brown, natives of the Indies. Between the two worlds were the Chinese, some poor, like coolies, but many clearly pretending to the status of Caucasians in wide brimmed European hats and jackets, often worn incongruously with traditional wide bottomed black Chinese trousers. A handful even drove motor cars to rival the Governor General's - especially those growing fat off lucrative government contracts. Wealthy Chinese could be extremely influenSitil and were second only to the Dutch in importance - and wealth. Few Europeans possessed houses which could match the 'palaces' of the rich Chinese. Here and there in the main European shopping areas, natives laden with bundles and parcels stacked them in the big and expensive carriages of wealthy Europeans and Chinese. A steam tram rattled past every fifteen minutes with passengers hanging out of the windows on each side. A khaki-clad policeman with a wide brimmed hat, turned up at one side, brought desultory order to the milling sados, carriages and pedestrians.

Van Es was no more interested in the Chinese than he was in the Inlanders - except the Indies women, of course. The Chinese were just willing and voluntary partners of the Dutch in their efforts to turn the Indies from a timeless, sleepy, tropical garden into a time-conscious, cost-conscious, vigorously exploited, effectively managed and profitable colony. Just as he had no Inlander friends, Van Es also had no Chinese friends, and didn't want any. Nobody in the service did. In their different ways, these two groups existed merely to serve the Dutch, and Dutchmen took an interest in them only to the extent that they needed guidance or, sometimes, a good kicKing, to be encouraged to do this. The Dutch ruled, the Chinese made the money and the Inlanders did the work.

As he walked about, Van Es's mind wandered back to last night's comment from the Colonel that he wanted to see him. He felt sure the meeting would be about promotion because the Colonel would not want to see him about much else. He resolved to try to make the appointment on Monday. But before then, loomed Saturday night and Sunday and a chance to again see Justina!

Van Es knew that he had to have his gameplan ready before he met her that night. Both of them would meet with expectations. They knew each other now, they knew that they were interested in each other, a step forward had to be taken and that step could be only in one direction. Van Es wanted her and, if she maintained her refusal to use one of Atek's rooms, then it was his villa or nothing. He must make up his mind about this before tonight. With Indies women one always had to be careful. Once they had their hooks into a man it could be difficult to shake them lose. Was Justina planning to hook him? Or would she just go home next morning like a good girl and wait to see if he wanted her again? The difficulty was that Van Es thought that she was capable of both.

She was pretty, easy-going, fun, willing to talk about herself, interested to ask questions and able to converse fluently in Dutch. It would be amazing if her only objective in life was to be a 'lady of the night'. While she had no formal education or money, nevertheless, she had assets which, if deployed carefully, could net her a male catch worth having and, perhaps, change her life very much for the better. The fact that she refused to be taken to a back room at Atek's showed clearly that she had a definite perception of her value and that she would not be led easily to devalue it. Her message had been clear. She was available. But if Van Es wanted her it would have to be on her terms.

But, Van Es reasoned to himself, these terms could not include any long term association with <u>him</u>. Surely she could not even be beginning to think along those lines! He, the Tuan besar and, she, the companion of all and any men who could afford her.

Inlanders understood their position well. But Justina was of mixed blood, a Eurasian, and the half-Europeans viewed themselves very differently, in fact often thought of themselves as full Europeans with all the habits and privileges implied.

Van Es sensed that Justina could be dangerous to a man who wanted no female attachments, yet craved the company and services of women. Yet he couldn't resist liKing her. With brother officers one could joke but not confide. With a woman one could confide, one could let down one's guard, be oneself, share thoughts and feelings. One need no longer be alone!

When he awoke from his customary afternoon siesta these thoughts welled up from Van Es's subconscious. He stretched out an arm across the empty bed. How different it would be if Justina's warm, lithe body was curled up beside him now!

3

Since he had met Justina, Van Es had not had other women. When Justina touched him and snuggled against him tonight, Van Es knew that he had no choice but to take her home. There was no point in staying late at Atek's.

"Come," he told her. Let's go to my place."

Between Senen and Weltevreden it was pitch black under the trees, but still they sat somewhat primly opposite one another in the back of a delman, each very well aware of the commitment which had now been made and of what lie ahead. The road was not asphalted here and the carriage wheels ground noisily against the hard but irregular surface.

At the villa, Sup was long ago asleep and, before entering the darkened house, they slipped off their shoes, Indies-style, on the veranda. Van Es walked behind her, lightly holding her arms, to guide her to the bedroom. Even before he could shut the door behind him, Justina had swivelled round, thrown her arms around him and pressed her silky lips hungrily to his. Van Es returned her kiss greedily, all the while pushing her firmly backwards towards the bed. He felt her hands unbuttoning his tunic and he ripped open the buttons down the front of her blouse. Each tugged frantically to bring the other's top down over their shoulders. As Justina's knees buckled behind her, her hands had pulled open his belt and were busy urgently unbuttoning his trousers. Each tore at the other in a sizzling frenzy of frustrated lust. Van Es pushed up her long dress to around her hips while Justina herself deftly slipped off her thigh-length underwear, wriggled down quickly onto the flat of her back and spread her thighs urgently, so that Van Es could penetrate her easily. Van Es now held what Justina's long skirts and high-necked tops had concealed - soft but well shaped calves and thighs, a slender waist, firm breasts. The pupils of her eyes were very large and black against their whites and bore a look of craving expectancy. Penetrating her was so smooth that the moment he entered her Van Es felt it was like a coming home, a return to a place tailor-made for him, which it was natural for him to pierce and for her to receive. At the moment of penetration Justina clung to him frantically, closed her eyes and flung back her head.

"Oh, my god," she kept moaning, "Oh, my god!"

She ran her fingers repeatedly over his cropped

head and kissed his chest, Van Es kissed her lips, her little pointed tongue, her eyes, her throat, her milky breasts and sucked at her protruding nipples, making her moan even more. At the height of the storm he arched his back, pushing himself straight up on his arms and thrusting into her with deep, powerful thrusts. When she judged the time was right, Justina locked her arms behind his back in a grip of steel, crushing him into her, and, when it came, making his erection last for a delicious eternity. With a deep gasp of relief, Van Es lowered himself onto her like a floppy rag doll. Sweat poured off them, the pillows had been kicked on the floor, clothes were scattered everywhere. They had made love with demented savagery, the touch of their skins unlocking a flood of desires and pent-up emotions, like some frenzied mock battle between two amorous beasts of the jungle who had encountered each other, swayed and fought together, until finally collapsing exhausted, locked in each others arms amid the debris and carnage of their ferocious coupling. Van Es rolled to one side and lay quiet. Justina gently and contentedly stroked his head.

The whole night, Justina slept curled up in Van Es's arms. The moment he awoke, Van Es felt her shape against him and wanted her again. She was asleep and, as he turned her towards him, still drowsy, half awake and half asleep, she let him move her wherever he wanted and do whatever he liked. Then they slept again, their bodies entwined.

It was late when they finally woke up and despite the pleasure she had given him, Justina was still merely one of many young ladies who had slept in his bed. In Van Es's mind ladies of the night were best left to the night. When it was daylight he preferred that they went home. Usually, he did not even offer them breakfast. He left Justina to get up, while he went to the washroom behind the bedroom. He used a small dipper to throw water from a large tiled cistern over himself, which was so icy that he sucked in his breath. He felt hot and sweaty after his repeated exertions and soaped himself thoroughly, closing his eyes to keep the soap out. Thus blinded, he felt Justina's body suddenly behind him, pressing against him, felt her hands spreading the soap everywhere.

Now it was his turn to swivel round, to shower her with the icy water, so that she sucked in her breath with the sensual shock of it, and to spread the foamy soap over every nook and cranny of her body. Their kisses were another form of coupling. The douche became a mouth watering ecstasy which could only end in one way.. Van Es pulled her down onto the hard tiles and, while she gripped him with her thighs and arched her back, Van Es pushed into her again and again until they were both groaning with ecstasy. Drying each other perfunctorily, they stumbled back to the bed and slept again.

When they awoke, the sun was still shining but the shadows were lengthening. Seeing that Justina was awake, Van Es slipped his arm beneath her shoulders and hugged her to him. Justina nestled against him in the curve of his arm. Both now had a delicious sense of belonging to each other, of having exposed themselves to each other in the most intimate ways, making them somehow feel one.

"Tell me about yourself," he said.

"You know already," said Justina softly. 'There is not much to tell about someone like me."

"But your father was European!"

"Yes", said Justina sadly. "But he left a long time ago and my mother is just a simple woman. What can my life ever be?"

"You speak good Dutch. How did you learn?"

"At school, and from listening to my father and his friends - and now from my friends."

"Your friends! Do you have Dutch friends?"

"You are my friend", Justina said simply and perhaps with unintended pointedness.

How many times had Van Es heard women tell him that? He had thought that the two of them were talking as genuine friends but, in an instant, she had reminded him that she was the 'friend' of anyone who paid her. He felt their 'oneness' momentarily breaking down. He remained silent for a while but then hugged her involuntarily. After all, she was a woman and his arm was round her.

"There must be something you can do," he said reflectively, without much hope now that she would give an honest reply.

"I am doing something."

"No. I mean something respectable and worthwhile."

At last she answered him seriously.

"I had only a little schooling and, in any case, I was glad to leave."

"Why?"

"It was so humiliating. Every morning, even though I was half Dutch, I had to squat down with the children of Inlander officials to show respect to the Dutch teachers by walking past them in this squatting position. Even as a child I felt very demeaned."

Van Es felt a sense of guilt that he would not normally have felt. He knew the procedures in Dutch schools and, indeed, in other institutions. It was all very simple: The Dutch were advanced and the natives were backward. Of course, they should show respect to the white 'mothers' and 'fathers' who had come to live among them and help them! But now Justina was giving him an uncomfortable insight into her side of the experience.

"It is always good to show respect to superiors," he said tersely, but not unkindly.

Justina stayed silent.

"I would like to be respected like the Dutch," she said finally. "After all, I am part Dutch."

"Yes, you seem very Dutch. If it wasn't for your exotic colouring you could easily be mistaken for a Dutch girl."

Justina ran her fingers thoughtfully through the hairs on his chest.

"Am I more exotic than European?"

Van Es laughed.

"You are both, in the nicest possible way."

Justina fantasised:

"If I was really Dutch, I could ride in a big carriage like the grand ladies of Batavia, with servants to help me in and out; my husband would be respected and so would I. And, perhaps, I could go to Holland. I would really like to see Holland. The Dutch in Europe must have so much money. It must really be like paradise there!"

Van Es said nothing.

"It will be a shame if you cannot do something with your life," he said flatly.

"Maybe I will marry a big, strong, rich, Dutchman," said Justina, throwing an arm over his chest.

Van Es was not surprised.

"Like me?" he laughed.

"Like you," she giggled.

"You'd like that, I'm sure."

"Yes, because then I would be completely Dutch and not as, at the moment, half Dutch and half native. I would live in the Dutch world, which is so different from that of the Inlanders. I would have money and a nice house like this one. I would be in the Dutch network. I would have connections. Then I could do something with my life."

Justina lay back, pulling away from him, staring up at the wooden beams of the ceiling and spoke vehemently.

"I hate the backward ways of the Inlanders and I hate their poverty."

Van Es suddenly saw another side to Justina. She was not just soft and loveable. Not just out for a good time and a little money. She nursed deeply felt resentments and aspirations.

"I'm sorry," she said, sensing that she had been too frank and burying her head in his shoulder.

Van Es hugged her again. After all, she was a human being. Why shouldn't she want a better life?

He was pleased that she should share with him her most private thoughts and because she had his qualified sympathy, it renewed the sense of oneness he had felt when they first woke up.

Something made him turn his head towards. Her long, black eye lashes and the corners of her oval eyes were wet with tears. She had been crying quietly.

Van Es bent over her, gently kissed her tears and said tender things to her. Her tears were proof that he had truly reached her little heart and his kisses evidence that Justina had truly moved his!

As they had talked, the day had waned to evening! Night was on its way again! Van Es knew now that, against his golden rule, he would not be sending Justina home today. He felt closer to her than he usually did to his women. He had not only penetrated her body. He had succeeded in penetrating her intellect, her mind and her emotions. He felt that she had opened everything to him. Instead of asking her to leave, he called Sup and asked him to prepare rice, meat, vegetables and fruit so that they could catch up with their missed breakfast and lunch - as if he was entertaining a real friend. The girl was half Dutch and she should eat at a Dutchman's table like a Dutch woman!

The pair ate in the living room with Justina wearing her own blouse but one of Van Es's sarongs, which was much more comfortable than her skirt. Her long, jet, hair was held up loosely at the back by a clip, but not in a bun or anything tight like that, so that it still looked whispy and feminine. They didn't speak much but Justina served him with food and smiled at him with warm intimacy.

"May I have a fork and spoon," she asked suddenly.

Van Es looked across at her place and realised that Sup had assumed that she would eat native-style, with her fingers. He said nothing, but called:

"Sup, Sup, spoon, fork, cepat, cepat."

Justina smiled appreciatively and concentrated on her food.

"You should have a woman here to cook for you," she observed with a slow smile, as they ate, he, big, blonde, European and sitting four-square in one chair, she, petit, dark and Eastern in the other, one leg tucked up languidly beneath her.

"No. I don't need it," said Van Es. "Most nights I eat at the mess. I can get Dutch food there."

"Perhaps it is a wife you need, not a cook. Then you would stay at home more."

Van Es would have had to have been very stupid not to sense a trap.

He said flatly: "The barracks are usually a soldier's home. I'm privileged to have this place."

"But you do have it. Wouldn't you prefer a wife to look after you and to be able to live here more comfortably?"

Now it was Van Es's turn to reveal something of his true feelings. Justina had dominated his body. Now she impregnated his thinking with her thinking. Their thoughts, like their bodies earlier, were becoming entwined.

"Sometimes yes, sometimes no," Van Es said truthfully. "I'm not in a hurry to get married. There are too many ties and responsibilities."

Justina kept her eyes on her plate.

Van Es went on: "I like to be free. I wouldn't marry just so that I could be looked after and eat at home. Ja, but, then, sometimes I think it would be nice to have a family."

"Well, then! There you are," she said, seizing the opportunity offered.

Yes, but I am also a soldier and a soldier's life can be unpredictable and dangerous," said Van Es, withdrawing again behind his old attitudes and decisions. "Of course, I like women, but it doesn't mean I have to marry them."

"Maybe later," said Justina, raising her eyes from her plate to shoot him an inquisitive glance.

"Ja. Ja. Maybe later," said Van Es continuing to eat without looking up.

To Van Es, there was a world of difference between a prostitute and a girl friend. One didn't take prostitutes to the kind of places one took friends. In fact, one didn't make friends of prostitutes at all. Any more than prostitutes made friends of their customers. But, already, he had entered into a special relationship with Justina. He had not just had sex and immediately sent her home. He had talked to her for hours. He 'knew' her and, although he, himself would never use the word, had become 'involved' with her.

Although apprehensive about it, after the meal, Van Es still could not break the tie that bound them and took the highly unusual course of suggesting that they went together to Gambir where some young European men were showing off their skills riding new, motor powered, bicycles. Justina agreed and she was at once no longer just a paid sex worker but more a friend with whom he was about to share something.

The display was an incredible, if noisy, showing off of daredevil dexterity by some young tearaways. Wooden ramps sent the bikes and their riders high into the air before crashing down unstably onto a dusty track illuminated by blazing torches. Every time a bike took off a great gasp went up from the crowd. Even Van Es was impressed.

"Technology these days is moving very fast," he mused out loud. We already have the motor car but who would have thought that an engine could have been made small enough to power a bicycle!"

Van Es and Justina were standing close-by and the slender girl clung to his arm and made a mock-frightened face every time the cycles roared past.

Justina looked very pretty in her long, dark blue dress and white blouse, set off by a wide-brimmed, white, dress hat topped off with a sprig of feathers in muted colours. European-looking though she was, Van Es could never resist thinking that native women looked incongruous in large European hats, as if they were playing dress-up! He thought that Dutch people looked equally incongruous in Indies sarongs!

Apart from standing together to watch the displays, he and Justina walked without touching. Although they were only doing what friends might do, Van Es could not forget that Justina was a prostitute and might be recognised as such. From time to time she bumped deliberately against him or touched the tips of his fingers with her hand, to try to maintain the intimacy between them, as if she was scared of losing his interest. But Van Es was unresponsive and kept a distance between them, as if pretending that they were really not together.

The couple were by no means exceptions at Gambir because there were other Europeans there with their local ladies. But, Van Es didn't like to be seen with ladies like his because he wanted the fact that his girlfriends were prostitutes to be known to as few people as possible, preferably to himself alone. And while the military might encourage men to have local permanent housekeepers and even wives, prostitution had a different connotation and he sensed that for too many people to know his habits would do his career no good at all! Going to Gambir was a risk but, then again, senior officers rarely went there and it was only they that Van Es was really concerned about. Each military and bureaucratic rank followed a rigid code of demarcation and protocol and it was easy to predict where certain officers or officials would or would not be.

After the displays, there was a market of life's daily necessities, laid out on rickety wooden stalls, beneath hissing kerosene lamps. Many of the vendors were selling fruits, cooked foods and drinks. The Europeans, in their ubiquitous white clothes looked incongruous and other worldly in the darkness, amidst a gaggle of dark-skinned, bare foot, natives in sarongs and native headdress. Van Es quite liked walking amongst the natives like this. As a white man, as a Tuan besar, he knew his power and felt important. He could sense his importance in the black eyes of all who looked at him - or avoided looking. He could feel it in the respectful tones of their voices. It was good to be a white man in the

Indies. Sometimes, the native stares were curious, sometimes fearful. The glances he liked best were those from little brown girls with long black hair and laughing eyes, whose look often seemed a shy invitation! Yes! It was definitely good to be a white man among such women! He stopped to buy a cigar from a woman who sold assorted sizes from jars and raised her kerosene lamp high to set it alight. The woman smiled and nodded approvingly. Van Es inhaled proudly. Yes! It was great to be a white Tuan besar! One had only to give the command and anything, literally anything, could be had for the asking!

At the night market, most of the sellers were men and many of the bony-legged vendors had their wares slung from shoulder poles. There were sellers of meat, or satay, on a stick which they cooked to perfection by fanning a perpetually smouldering charcoal fire and then served with chopped onions and peanut sauce. Each vendor had two large baskets attached to either end of a shoulder pole; in one was the stove and kitchen utensils, in the other the supplies and, often, even a miniature wooden stool on which customers could sit.

"Would you like some?" said Justina, nodding at some satay.

Van Es made a face.

"Not for me. I never eat from hawkers. I don't want to get sick. Anyway, we've already had a good lunch."

Secretly, Van Es didn't want <u>her</u> to eat there. Eating like that would have been highly embarrassing for a Dutch military officer. Definitely not done!

With nothing else to do, they went back to their love nest, threw off their clothes and lay together again - this time tenderly and lovingly and without the frenzy of yesterday. But, later that night, Van Es was sure that Justina really must go home. She didn't want to go. She snuggled up to him and tried everything she could to get him to change his mind.

"Don't you like me?" she asked, pouting delectably.

Van Es's mouth dried at the sight of her and at the renewed touch of her. In an ideal world, the last thing he wanted was that she should go. But, he said, matter-of-factly:

"I have my duty to do."

"So, you really don't like me?" Justina tested.

"Ja, of course, I like you," he said with feigned irritation. "I like you very much. But I must work tomorrow. We'll meet again at Atek's."

"When? Tomorrow night?"

"Maybe. I don't know yet. I can't promise. Maybe on Wednesday. Let's say Wednesday."

Accepting the inevitable, as Justina left the villa to walk down the short path to a waiting sado, she quickly and briefly stepped back into the house to give him a last, lingering, kiss. Then, looking longingly over her shoulder at him as she walked, she let her fingers slide gently and tantalisingly out of his, as if she left with an extreme reluctance which he could easily remedy by grasping her hand and drawing her back. But there was no drawing back, and after she had gone and Van Es returned to the bedroom, he felt inexpressibly lonely! Instead of being a disinterested purchaser who had bid farewell

GABRIELSE

to a disinterested supplier what had genuinely become one had been brutally ripped apart! When he tried to sleep her image and the memory of her touch tortured him. He tossed this way and that way, face down, face up and still the touch of her and the smell of her haunted him. Her perfume was everywhere - in the pillows, in the sheets. In the twilight of semi-consciousness, before a restless sleep finally claimed him, Van Es found himself whispering her name like an animal whose mate had been suddenly and cruelly snatched away.

By morning, Justina was temporarily forgotten. Instead of whispering Justina's name Van Es found his thinking dominated by Colonel Hogendorp's invitation to make an appointment to discuss his "future." Filled with a new optimism about his prospects, he hurried to his office with unusual alacrity, yelling commandingly at the native 'babus' (general name for servants) for his morning coffee as he strode past the pantry en route to the desk he knew would be piled high with files. His sharp eyes rapidly scanned the desk-top for urgent messages but there were none. He walked to open a side door into the office where his male secretaries worked. As soon as they saw him the men snapped to attention and wished him a good morning more or less in unison. He addressed the soldier nearest the door.

"Sergeant. Put a call through to Colonel Hogendorp's office for me."

Almost as soon as he returned to his desk the black telephone rang and he was speaking to Colonel Hogendorp's adjutant, Captain Janszen. He explained what had happened at the Club.

"Sorry, Major. The Colonel's on a month's tour of inspection in Java."

Van Es was shocked. His expectations had been raised and his surprise turned quickly to disappointment.

"You've no idea what he wants me for? he asked dejectedly.

"None at all, Major. I can only suggest that you try again when he gets back."

Of course! What else! Van Es put the receiver down slowly and rocked backwards and forwards, with his chair standing on its two back legs only, his chin resting lightly on the tips of his fingers. Then he let the chair's front legs bang down onto the floor again. Life had to go on!

As usual, his in-tray was piled high with files from various units which he would have to read, write his response and send on along the line. Not being able to reach the Colonel had made him less than enthusiastic about dealing with the files but, today, he had a reprieve. After last week's stock-taking and audit he had to make an inspection of the military godowns at Sunda Kelapa and Tanjung Priok so today he would be out of the office all day. Perhaps tomorrow, too. Having done nothing that morning except make his disappointing phone call, Van Es took up his high, white helmet and left the office once more, as usual, locking the door behind him. There were always sados waiting outside the barracks and, as he lolled in the back, his good humour began to return.

Like every day in the tropics, it was a beautiful day to be out and about, and Batavia was a beautiful city through which to drive. Everywhere there were shady and, sometimes, colourful trees and shrubs - Waringin trees of fantastic shapes, Travellers Ferns, blade-leafed palms, trees with delicate white Melati flowers, some of which dropped every day, others with flaming red blossoms, some with clusters of delicate pink flowers. It was like living in an exotic forest. In fact, Java was widely known as the 'Garden of the East.' The little sado creaked and swayed northwards along the wide, packed-earth roads, shaded everywhere by the leafy, green trees.

Compared to Holland, Van es always thought that, not only Koningsplein, but everything else in Batavia had been laid out and built on a gigantic scale, as if space was endless. Three hundred years before, he knew that his ancestors had razed even the smallest vestiges of native occupation of Batavia and, since then, had regarded the whole area as a blank sheet on which to make bold urban and architectural statements reflecting the grand imperial design.

As they rattled along through Waterlooplein and past the Concordia Club, with its iron tables set out under the trees on the lawns at the front, for a while he could watch the massive, white, three storey, Empire-style, government headquarters building recede into the distance. They passed Wilhemina Park (present Istiqual Mosque area) with its bridges and fountains and public benches where people could rest tranquilly in the heart of the busy city. The grand palace of the Governor General where he had attended the Queen's Birthday Ball was easily the most spectacular of all the buildings with its colonnaded portico, looking like a shimmering Greek temple in the midst of the exotic vegetation of a lush tropical park.

In fact, this part of Batavia was in truth one huge park with the bright, white, fairy-tale, neo-classical palaces, offices, barracks, churches and homes of the Dutch colonisers dotted here and there, each set well back from the road in its own gigantic plot of land and each with a row of low, white-plastered, brick pillars at the front linking a ubiquitous single-chain fence. Even the bridges over the many canals which intersected Batavia were white. The lamp standards were white. The grand hotels which he soon saw on his way north along the Molenvliet (the present Jalan Hayam Wuruk) from the Harmonie Club were white. And, apart from police and certain military units, hardly a European man or woman passed who was not dressed from head to toe in shimmering white. Even the Government's native staff had to wear white tunics above their colourful sarongs. Batavia had truly earned its sobriquet as the Queen City of the East, thought Van Es complacently.

They drove now along the long, straight, canalised River Ciliwung, here and there bamboo rafts being polled down to the sea or large groups of chattering women washing clothes from steps leading down into the water. Groups of laughing boys dived in and out while small girls immersed themselves more sedately at the water's edge. The eastern bank was not such a pretty sight as the west but, fortunately, the messy, unplanned, native quarter there with its many mills and other industries was substantially shielded from view by thick trees.

His driver maintained a cracking pace through the traffic of carriages passing too and fro along this main artery. Soon, they passed the great, ornamented home of the Captain China, who represented and spoke for the hoards of Chinese who had settled in the heart of the business district; and then the rows and rows of densely built Chinese shophouses which looked as if they had been moved bodily from South China and plonked down in Batavia.

The city was entered from north or south by giant, plastered brick, white archways which would not have looked out of place as dedications to conquering generals in classical Rome. And then they were in the commercial hub of Batavia, with its huge, neo-classical, imperial buildings.

The grand canal or Kali Besar was filled with flat- bottomed lighters with tall masts and sails, discharging their cargoes into sheltered pavilions from which armies of sweating, native coolies hauled them away to nearby godowns. Behind the pavilions, across the usual wide road, were the offices of the trading, shipping, insurance and banking companies which were at the heart of Batavia's success.

Van Es' heart soared with pride at the sight of some of the older, more nondescript, buildings giving way to fine, modern structures with towers and cupolas befitting a great and successful Oriental emporium. Almost every time he went there an old building seemed to have disappeared and a new one stood in its place. The streets here were crowded with Dutch, Chinese and natives, walking, riding in carriages, and some on pedal cycles.

Very few of the godowns he had come to inspect were new. Most of the long, narrow, warehouses with their white walls and red tiled roofs, had been there for two centuries or more. But they did the job, so there was no need to waste money replacing them! For the next few hours Van Es was so busy that he forgot to take lunch. The storehouse keeper eventually got so much on his nerves with his concern that "Tuan must eat" that Van Es agreed to stop and eat a plate of rice thoughtfully prepared for him by a woman so old that she looked as if she mightn't live to serve another one. The Inlanders seemed obsessed with food and not only never missed their own but thought it very unhealthy for someone else to do so.

Van Es continued into the afternoon, checking this and that and making notes in a small pocket book, the contents of which he would later transcribe into his files. It was cool and dark inside the godowns so he was mercifully spared the full impact of the noon heat. There were usually numerous mistakes in the storekeeper's tallies and one check was rarely enough. Van Es knew he would be back again next day, and perhaps even the next and the next. It depended.

There was no time in one day to go both to Sunda Kelapa, the name of the area around the old port of Batavia, and also the eight miles to Tanjung Priok. Van Es had never intended this because it was faster and more comfortable to reach Tanjung Priok by train. And it was refreshing to get out of the city, however pleasant it might be - to rattle through the flooded Sawah Besar or great rice field to the south east, to watch the paddy farmers up to their knees in mud, at work with their wooden ploughs and water buffalo in the glistening wet rice fields fringing the sea, to see the ramshackle but quaint-looking little thatched bamboo huts on stilts where the farmers lived, and to think or even to daydream as they train rocked and rolled along the long, straight railway track, lined with dense jungle but here and there dotted with coconut palms and orchards. Like all Dutchman, Van Es didn't allow himself to be carried away too much with the work which had to be done. He may have had to be reminded to eat lunch but he needed no reminder to stop work at 4 p.m. sharp.

Back at the villa, it was too late for his usual siesta and, after a refreshing douche in cold water, Van Es made his way to the mess, not so much to eat as to wash away the trials of the day with a few beers. In the cool of the evening the streets seemed to be even more full of people than in the scorching day-time and he passed many little knots of people clustered around street vendors, like the satay makers, selling the evening meal. Everyone was always very relaxed and happy as they squatted down at the roadside or beneath the trees. In the darkness, they were often only vague shapes, illuminated now and then by a flickering flame or lamp.

Evenings at the mess were in some ways therapeutic because it was here that one could moan and groan openly into sympathetic ears about the trials and tribulations of the day - about how stupid the natives seemed, about the need to check and re-check everything, about the inordinate amount of time it all took, and so on and so on.

By the time he reached the mess, Van Es felt jaded by the day's events. It had been a long and frustrating day, lunch had been well meant but inadequate, he had failed to obtain any good news from the Colonel or even to reach the Colonel and, as night drew closer, Justina and the prospect of a lonely night in his dark house, began to dominate his mind. In the heat of passion he had begun to think himself in love with Justina but tonight Van Es felt irritated with himself for thinking such a thing! Justina was a prostitute! How could a senior colonial officer possibly fall in love with a prostitute! The whole thing was absurd and he had been very stupid! Yet, since meeting Justina, he had felt a loneliness he had not felt before, a loneliness that deepened the more he felt he had an attachment to her. In the past, after he had finished with a prostitute, he did not feel lonely! Life went on as before, with days spent at the Commissary, evenings at the mess or Club and early weekday nights to enable him to be up by 5 a.m. The women in his life satisfied a periodic male need, that was all. Justina had done that, too. Yet, for some reason, he could not just toss her away. Was his fascination solely that he could talk to her like a friend?

"What madness", he thought to himself. Justina had said herself that she had only a little schooling so, how much talking could she do. She had told him about herself, but that hardly qualified as conversation. Surely, very soon, she would run out of things to say. Would he be attracted to her then? Of course not! He told himself that he had to get a grip on his feelings and downing more and more beer with his friends he made up his mind unequivocally that he would not rush to see Justina again. He had said that he would try to see her on Wednesday and he would stick to that. In fact, since he had this uneasy feeling of 'involvement' with her, maybe it would be better if he didn't see her again even on Wednesday. And maybe he should get Justina out of his system by picking up another woman somewhere else!

Van Es was fairly tipsy when he arrived home and lay down to sleep. Usually after a drinking session at the Club he slept easily. But not tonight. Even if he tried to shut Justina out of his thoughts, his body remembered her, remembered her shape and her softness and wanted her. Once again he tossed and turned until he could stand it no longer. He dressed again and had himself driven to Atek's. Maybe she would be there! It was worth a try. In his tortured state he had not thought out what would happen if she was there. Would he break yet another golden rule and take her home on a weekday night? Or would they just sit close and talk?

At Atek's, he looked around, his eyes darting into every dark corner, but Justina was not there.

"Selamat malam, Tuan," a girl's voice said somewhere to his right, before a hand touched his arm lightly.

It was Justina! Van Es spun around. No. It was not Justina! It was Siti!

Van Es was momentarily off balance.

"Oh," he said, "it's you."

"Are you loo?"

"No, Tuan, not tonight. But I will tell her that I saw you. She is my friend."

Van Es had no interest in remaining at Atek's without Justina so he returned home. More tired than ever now, this time, he fell asleep quickly.

Next day, Van Es told himself that he was glad Justina hadn't been at Atek's because now he had time to get her out of his system. "My God! She had even talked about marriage!" He spent a second day again at Sunda Kelapa but in the evening there was a party at the Concordia and he joined in with gusto. He used his hot and tiring trips outside the office as the excuse for heavy drinking and that night could hardly remember staggering home from the officers mess! On Wednesday, the routine was the same but he found that he could hardly drink! His heart wasn't in it. Once again his mind had returned to Justina. The problem with Wednesday was that he knew for sure that she would be waiting for him! He knew that if he went to her, he could have her. Her pale skin, her shining dark hair, her bright eyes, her real or feigned affection for him, the 'sympathy' they shared together - Van Es was obsessed. His concentration crumbled, he lost track of what people were saying around him and re-joined the conversation at the wrong times giving ridiculous comments and replies.

"You're in a bad way Van Es," a friend said, semi-humourously.

"He's either sick or in love," joked another.

"Either way the only cure is for him to go

straight home to bed!"

The whole bar roared with coarse laughter at this but Van Es knew that they were right and, signing his chit, he made his way directly to Atek's. He did not hurry because, until the last, he wanted to hope that Justina meant nothing to him. But he could not linger because mind and body were driving him inexorably to her!

The moment Van Es saw Justina again he felt better, felt good, felt himself laugh ing lightly and felt himself holding her close. He had ordered a beer and sat down at a table, where Justina joined him. Last week, he had simply wanted to take her home to make love. This week, he wanted to do the same thing but, looking around he inexplicably felt the squalor of the surroundings keenly, felt that his relationship with Justina had outgrown Atek's and, indeed, was cheapened by it. He wanted to do something with her, to share something with her that was typical of the doings and sharings of normal couples, as opposed to those who met in houses of ill repute late at night. But what to do? Where to take her? Incredibly, Justina seemed to have a similar idea because she suddenly said:

"They have dancing at the Hotel des Indes to-night. I have never been but I would very much like to go."

The Hotel des Indes! Dancing! Exposure to the full public gaze! Van Es's thoughts raced. She had articulated something along the lines of his own musings but dare he do it. She dare, of course, What had she to lose by being seen in an elegant hotel with a European officer. But what about him. Dare he be seen at an elegant hotel with a girl who might be recognised as a prostitute?

"I don't really feel like dancing," he lied, to try to dissuade her.

"I would just like to see, that's all," said Justina cleverly. "We don't have to dance if you don't want to."

Van Es thought that here was a possibility! To visit the hotel and just watch; not to be on full public display! He weighed the short-term options for his evening. If they did not go to the hotel they would have to either stay where they were or go to his villa. Tonight, he didn't fancy staying where they were. And although it was far from being the case that he didn't want to take her home, something made Van Es feel that Justina was good enough to be taken somewhere better than Atek's. And it would be he, Van Es, the Tuan besar, who would introduce this lowly Indies girl to the glittering social life at a great hotel. The Hotel des Indes was along the Molenvliet, not far from the Harmonie Club and was famous for its dances. New music was sweeping in from Europe and, while official balls remained staid, the younger generation went wild to the strains of the avande garde, happy-go-lucky melodies. He would almost have preferred to have revealed to her the magical new world of the movies at the Schouwburg (present Gedung Kesenian), but a cinema audience might contain friends and acquaintances from whom one could hide during the darkness of the screening but who could be met entering, leaving or during the highly social intermission!

"We'll go to des Indes," Van Es decided.

Justina turned elatedly, flung her arms around his neck and gave him a playful kiss.

They drove over by delman, as before, sitting facing one another but, this time, with their knees touching affectionately. Once again, each had the feeling of being one person, of being one person sharing, of doing something which they had discussed and both agreed to do, of executing their joint will. They were a couple! Justina's eyes were wide with wonder as the black carriage pulled into the driveway of the brilliantly lit hotel. When the delman stopped, Justina prepared to alight, but barefoot doorman in sarongs and Java hats ran forward to assist her by taking her hand. At first, Justina looked a little unsure of herself, but Van Es smiled up at her and her confidence returned. Both were conscious of suspicious stares from the hotel staff but Van Es, inured with the confidence of command and of being a member of the ruling power, walked forward with supreme confidence, passing his jaunty, flat, boater to a valet and showing Justina where to deposit her own hat. They were an arresting couple, dressed completely in white, but, he tall, well built and blond and she, slight, well-shaped but with an exotic darkness superimposed onto her pale, almost fragile-looking skin. They were not attending anything formal, like a ball, and so there was no fear of presentations or any other formality. And, although not as grand as the palace or even the two leading Clubs, the ballroom at des Indes was huge, and, filled by the kind of large and boisterous crowd there tonight, it was not impossible to be reasonably inconspicuous - especially since Van Es was not in uniform. Waiters, with white tutup jackets over their sarongs and black pecis on their heads, hurried round with drinks, while a small orchestra kept the young crowd whirling around the dance floor in an hysteria of gaiety. Justina looked quite at home among this sophisticated crowd in her long, capacious, white dress and frill, white blouse. The only item she lacked was a pair of evening gloves. Her black eyes shone and danced with excitement.

"Just one dance," she pleaded quietly, squeezing his arm. "Please."

To please her, he agreed, and the two whirled off around the dance floor and were quickly indistinguishable from the scores of other exhilarated couples enjoying the evening fun. Justina danced with gusto and, once he'd warmed up, Van Es found himself having a good time too. Again, it was largely because he felt that although he was dancing with Justina, she, too, was dancing with him. They were both contributing to a joint achievement. They were together. They were a couple. And he was not as afraid as he would have been had she been a Dutch girl because he knew he still had the power to say "goodbye" to her at any moment. After all, even for this, he would still be paying! She must do exactly what he told her and nothing more or less. She was his creature totally. And, unlike respectable Dutch ladies, he felt he had no need to fear that she would immediately be manoeuvring him towards a permanent, legal union! True, she had mentioned marriage at the villa but Van Es interpreted this as strictly conversational. Prostitutes like Justina didn't dream of marriage to high ranking Dutch officers!

The des Indes consisted of a main building plus a rambling assortment of bungalows and chalets in extensive, treed grounds. Hot from the dancing, the two strolled out into the hotel gardens, stopping when the lighted ballroom seemed far in the distance and where they were quite alone. Although they had been in physical contact all evening, each longed to press fully against the other and in doing so, in the shadows, beneath the great trees, they kissed passionately. Van Es wanted to kiss her. Justina wanted to show her gratitude! It was very late and the kiss encouraged them to give in completely to the desires of their bodies and return together to Van Es's villa, where their love making was as passionate but sweeter than before. It was midweek so Justina could not be allowed to stay all night. This time, as she lightly allowed her fingers to slip from his on the veranda, Van Es felt more desolate than ever, more like calling her back than ever. But it was impossible, and he let her go. He could only have a few hours sleep as it was.

"I will look for you on Saturday," she called softly as she glided into the night.

On Friday, Van Es made the long journey to

Tanjung Priok, as at Sunda Kelapa, spending a tedious day checking godown stocks. Knowing that he would see Justina again on Saturday he had no anxiety about her and enjoyed a carefree evening at the mess. In the office he talked only of boring, day-to-day matters, such as commodity prices and supplies or problems with suppliers. But, in the mess, the conversation was about more interesting topics, such as, dominion and politics, the latest government announcements, military actions throughout the Indies, punishments for deserters, postings, garrison expansions, structural changes, which officers were doing what and, of course, about Van Es's favourite topic, promotion!

In a sense it was a narrow, claustrophobic life and, for Europeans, over and above their duties, there was little to do - except have fun at the endless parties and dances, or with Batavia's ladies of the night. One good thing that could be said about life in Batavia was that the social life was far better even than in Holland! The Dutch expatriates were an alien group in a foreign country and felt that they had to cling together. In clinging, they had established a breathless calendar of opportunities for certain kinds of enjoyment. There was a seemingly endless sequence of receptions, breakfasts, lunches, dinners, soirees and dances. For those with the interest, which would not have included Van Es or many that he knew, Batavia's lonely cultural outpost at the Schouwburg managed to offer not only films but comedy and dramas, often performed by the city's amateur groups. While Van Es craved promotion, he was not always sure that he wanted a posting to Java or to an outlying island because, however limited the capital's cultural activities, the social life in the outstations might be vastly inferior! He had heard that some stations were nothing but outright boring with a routine that hardly varied day in and day out. For some of the Dutch who lived inland, a trip to Batavia or even to Surabaya or Semarang, Java's other big Dutch cities, was like a return to civilisation! Like so much else in Van Es's life, his thoughts and aspirations were riddled with contradictions! He felt he wanted the glory and perceived prospects of being a field officer yet would he enjoy life without the girls of Senen!

On Saturday morning he played soccer, as usual, and in the afternoon did little except sleep and while away the time until he could dine at the mess before making his way to Atek and Justina.

Justina had gone to Atek's alone the night before. She avoided entanglement with any of the men there and spent most of the evening telling Siti about her hopes of Van Es.

"He has a house," she told her friend.

"He must be very rich then," said Siti. "Considering that soldiers are always poor, you must be very lucky."

"At least he has the house."

"And no wife?"

" No wife."

"Is he looking for a wife?"

"He says "yes" and "no."

" Do you think he would take girls like us for a wife?"

"Why not? Men do."

"But he is a senior officer and you said he may be promoted."

"I think he likes me. He said I am the first women to ever stay the whole night at his place."

Siti hugged her affectionately and giggled.

"I cannot say much to him because I don't speak Dutch," she said wistfully. "You are lucky again."

"Much good it's done me so far," said Justina.

"Oh, come on! I'm sure he likes you more than the rest of us because he can talk to you. Perhaps you seem more like a European to him."

"Maybe."

"He must be really smitten with you because he came here looking for you the other night when you were not here."

"Did he?" said Justina with round-eyed astonishment, a smile spreading slowly across her face. "The trouble is that he's afraid of marriage", said Justina, focusing on the nub of her interest in Van Es."

"That's difficult."

"We'll see."

On Saturday night, Van Es turned up at Atek's earlier than ever, but this time he wanted to stay awhile before returning to the villa. He had tasted Justina now and taking her to bed wasn't quite as urgent as it had been the first time. They drank, hugged, laughed and enjoyed the music until Van Es suddenly became serious and asked:

"Where do you live?"

He was genuinely curious about the kind of house she lived in, her family, etcetera. Justina was as sharp as a needle and had no intention of diminishing herself in his eyes by answering truthfully. The fact of the matter was that, like many Inlanders, she lived in a hut made of woven bamboo walls, with a red tiled roof rather like a smaller version of Atek's place. The little house was located in one of a maze of alleys lined with similar sun-scorched, rickety-looking structures. Once Justina's father had left, family life reverted entirely to Indies ways and her mother and sisters merged steadily into the Inlander host society. Justina was the odd one out because she stubbornly refused to give up her Dutch heritage. She was known as the 'Dutch girl' of the family and often came into conflict with her mother when she accused her of letting her 'standards' drop.

Her mother had no such perceptions. She had been born an Inlander and would always remain an Inlander and she lived her life the way all Inlanders did. As far as she was concerned the family were Inlanders who had enjoyed a brief interlude with a Dutchman, whose presence made very little difference anyway because the family and home were always managed by the mother who inevitably stamped it indelibly with Indies ways. Justina had two younger sisters and the fact that they were four women in a family without men was a great sorrow and hardship to her mother. She knew what Justina did to make money and accepted it calmly as God's will. To her mind, it might have been regrettable under other circumstances but, as things were, there was nothing to be done about it. Anyway, was she herself any less of a prostitute for sleeping unmarried with the same man for two tours of his duty.

Justina had more men but didn't it amount to the same thing! Whatever the women did and however they did it, it was all in the cause of money and survival. She, too, came from an impoverished family and a large one, too. It had helped her and her family a lot that a white man had taken her on. He had paid for the house and without him who knows whether they would have had even that! Like many Indies women, she was a hard working and capable business person and had tried to train her daughters in the same mould. Even when her husband was still around, she had bought and sold at the market and she and Justina's younger daughters were still buying and selling and struggling to make ends meet from their own efforts. It had to be like that. No one was likely to help them.

Justina, on the other hand, felt that her Dutch blood was an advantage which should be exploited. She felt that her relative fluency in everyday Dutch was an asset that should be turned to advantage. And she felt that, although she had little education, she was not a stupid girl and therefore could hold her own socially even with a white Tuan besar! She looked good, she spoke Dutch well and she knew how to give a man a good time! Why not, then, try to marry a white man! Her mother had merely lived with her man who had eventually abandoned her. But, if Justina, could marry her man, she would have security and, who knew, maybe she would even end up amid the unimaginable riches of Holland! Why not? It could happen. It could be made to happen. It just needed the right man! And now there was Van Es! Was he the right man? Could he be manoeuvred into being the right man?

One thing she knew for sure. If Van Es realised how she really lived he would never marry her. There was very little furniture in the house, which they shared with her mother's old mother. The floors were bare, except for rattan mats which were put down for eating and sleeping. They prepared their food on the floor, ate on the floor and slept on the floor. Justina wore European dress when she went out at night because it was, in effect, her working uniform. But in the daytime she and all the members of her family wore the colourful Indies sarong and baju, drew drinking water from a well and bathed and washed their clothes in the canal. Justina had a wooden box in which she lay flat her 'uniform' clothes, taking them out only when she needed them and never leaving them around carelessly where they could be dirtied or damaged. The Dutch loved white and Justina had a number of dazzling white garments. But it was very difficult to keep white clean in the circumstances in which she lived. Luckily the Kali Baru, or new canal, was close by and the clothes could be washed there regularly.

Van Es asked again, "Where do you live?"

"In a house," she said innocently.

"You know, a house with rooms for eating and sleeping."

"Brick or bamboo?"

"Of course, brick," she lied.

Very few Inlanders lived in brick houses. These were reserved for the Dutch and the wealthy Chinese. Inlanders could only peer enviously from beyond the chain fences or through the trees at the life of privilege lived by the Dutch upper classes and the Chinese. The life of the Inlander, or lowest class, was lived among tumble- down, bamboo huts, more often than not outside! They defecated outside, washed outside, de-liced each other's hair outside, often ate outside from the warungs or by buying food from the itinerant coolies, rested outside in the cool of the evenings, children played games outside, teenage boys ogled teenage girls and older people relaxed at the doors of their homes in the cool of the evening chatting amongst themselves or to the many neighbours who lived close by. Bare foot, country clothes, no education, no money. This was the life of the Inlander - a life that Dutch tourist books described as 'magical.'

Van Es went on to ask her who lived at her house and Justina told him truthfully, but embroidered her replies until she thought he had the image almost of a respectable but poor European family doing the things European families do. Yet she stressed how hard it was to maintain a 'proper standard' and emphasised how much she longed to be part of a Dutch household once again.

"I like your house very much," she said.

Van Es smiled and hugged her close.

"Shall we go there now?"

Van Es was a little drunk and felt happy. He wanted to take her home but he had the taste for beer, too.

"One more beer first," he said.

Justina affected a gaiety she hardly felt, nervous as his question had made her. Though all she really wanted was to be with him at the villa, she didn't want him to probe her lifestyle any more and encouraged him to have several more glasses in quick succession so that he would forget any difficult questions and concentrate on enjoying himself.

"Shall we go back?" she repeated eventually, her hands clasped loosely around his neck and brushing his lips tantalisingly with her own.

"Ja, Ja, let's go back," said Van Es finally and good naturedly. "It's time to go."

Sexually, Justina was as attentive to him as she had been before, perhaps more so. She did everything she could to give him variety and prolong his pleasure. While he lay satiated and more than a little inebriated, Justina sponged his sweating body where he lay so that Van Es could feel the cool, damp, cloth soothing his skin. Eventually, he fell asleep and, not having been asked to leave, Justina sensed a victory had been won and that a routine had been established - hopefully. Next morning, she was up early and freshened herself before he awoke. She worked with Sup to prepare his usual breakfast but, when she heard him begin to move about, she took it to him herself on a bamboo tray which, once he had moved to a wicker chair, she served to him on her knees, in the Javanese tradition.

This Sunday he trusted her to be left alone in the house while he went to church. He had missed the service the previous week but felt that he could not afford to do so twice in a row. Everyone else went, especially senior officers, so, it was important to be seen there too. When he came back, Justina had prepared some light refreshments.

"This is just like being married." Van Es joked.

Justina smiled.

A man could easily get used to having a loving woman around, Van Es thought to himself. Suppose they really were married? It would be good while it lasted! But it needn't last forever! One day he'd go back to Holland and, if he was tired of her, she would stay in Batavia. Even if he wasn't tired of her he could hardly take her back to the Netherlands! That would be unthinkable! If he abandoned her, while she might be angry, she would be stuck in the Indies and he would be far, far away in Europe. Indies women could be very bitter and even dangerous when abandoned. There were plenty of tales about healthy Dutchman keeling over dead even before their ships reached Amsterdam because of the black magic of the Indies. Van Es wondered if Justina knew anything about black magic, about spells that could drive a man crazy, about plants that could poison and kill! Probably not, he thought. After all she was more European than Inlander. She probably knew as little as he did about the black arts. He hoped so!

As they lay side by side on the bed together that afternoon, Van Es turned on his side to examine her profile. Her eyes were closed, long, black lashes laying lightly on her cheek. Her lips were slightly parted. Her nose was small and cute. Her hair a black cloud on the pillow. It was too hot for covers and Van Es's eyes moved downwards over her round, soft breasts, her belly button and flat stomach, to the surprisingly thin hair at her groin an, finally, along her beautiful thighs to her feet. On her left ankle she wore a little gold chain. Van Es sighed. She was very beautiful and innocent looking and he couldn't imagine her angry - or ready to kill! She turned to him abruptly, looking him full in the eyes and draping an arm languidly around his shoulders.

"Do you love me," she asked. "Say you love me."

"I do love you," said Van Es thoughtlessly. "I love you very much."

Justina turned her head away and closed her eyes, pulling him on top of her with the arm that had been draped so apparently harmlessly around his shoulders. They did not kiss but she opened herself completely to him and held him tightly while he moved inside her.

"Let's get married," she whispered, her head thrown back with pleasure. "Let's get married.

Van Es' back was arched as far as it could arch and he let out a great sigh as he flooded inside her.

"I love you," he said, clinging to her more tightly than ever.

Justina stroked his hair gently as he lay on top of her, until they eventually rolled apart and, as usual, fell asleep.

On Sunday, once more Van Es left her in the house alone while he went to church. This week, the service made him feel a little uneasy. The minister began by saying how pleased he was to see his church more and more full and especially to see so many Dutch ladies there. It provided a growing opportunity, he said, for Dutchmen in the Indies to enjoy relationships and married life with women who were their racial, cultural and intellectual equals. Certain things had happened of necessity in the past, he went on, but the time was ripe to halt the erosion of racial purity in the Indies and especially to ensure that children were not exposed to what he called the unsavoury practices of the Indies babus (servants). Not comforting words for a man who had just fallen into a deep relationship with an Indies woman, albeit a woman of mixed blood! Van Es felt tension creeping up his neck and twisted his head from side to side in order to relax. He was glad when the service was over and he could return to Justina.

Justina had prepared a meal of rice, meat, vegetables and fruit the like of which he had never seen at the villa before. Before he left, she had asked him for a little money to buy food and while he was away a line of vendors with their foods hanging from baskets on shoulder poles, had trooped on and off the veranda. Justina could not help but sense that, this morning, for the first time in her life she was behaving like a true Dutch mevrouw (wife)! The ragged vendors were very respectful as the squatted down on the planks of the wooden veranda. Justina took her time to select the finest foods, savouring every second of her position and power. Then she doled out to each one appropriate sums of the money Van Es had given her.

The villa really didn't have a kitchen, as such, more a space at the back where battered pots were kept and, if necessary, food could be cooked. Van Es's limited supply of Dutch crockery and cutlery was kept in a cupboard in the living room, beside the dining table. Justina used Sup as her assistant and prepared for the two of them a meal that was less than a riysttavel but still plentiful and mouth-wateringly good.

Van Es roared with laughter when he saw the meal.

"I was only spoiled rotten like this by my mother," he told her.

Sup helped Justina lay out the food on the veranda and Justina served Van Es with whatever he wanted. He was a white king, coddled and served by two charming, smiling, black-eyed, bare foot, natives either of whom would fulfil his every whim. Van Es ate, European style, in one of the wicker chairs with a comfortable batik cushion. Justina sat, apparently submissively, curled up at his feet, on the hard floor. From time to time he stopped eating to stroke her shining, thick, hair. While they ate, a vendor approached selling batik.

"May we look?" asked Justina with an excited smile. "Look, he has some wonderful patterns."

In seconds, the veranda was covered with hand-made and decorated batik cloths of indescribable colour and in many intricate designs and patterns, all reflecting the rural inspiration of the women craftsmen who drew and painted them by hand. A pair of equally colourful rice birds flitted playfully, like young lovers, among the branches of the shady tree which overhung the veranda. Justina wrapped several of the flowery batik sheaths around her before she found one that she liked.

"May I please have this one?" she pleaded with an almost shy smile, standing with one leg slightly forward so that the sarong was displayed to its very

best advantage.

"Ja. Have it. Why not?" said Van Es with unaccustomed generosity. After all, he had bought her nothing as yet and the cost of the batik, beautiful though it was, was relatively small. The vendor left with his heavy baskets swaying on either side of him as he plodded on to the next prospect and Justina kept on the sarong she had bought. After lunch, they felt sleepy, as usual.

"Come, let's lie down for a while," said Van Es commandingly, getting up and pushing her playfully in front of him through the house to the bedroom.

Justina had wound the sarong tightly so that it clung revealingly to her buttocks and thighs, forcing her to take tiny steps.

Van Es laughed.

"You look like an Inlander woman in that sarong but it's very sexy," he said, alternatively massaging her buttocks or holding her hips as she walked.

As they entered the bedroom, Justina put one hand behind her and pulled his head round to kiss him passionately on the lips. Van Es was caressing the sheath of the sarong longingly. He tried to untuck it at the waist but Justina had folded it oddly and he couldn't manage it. Instead he began to role up the tight fitting garment.

"No. Don't," said Justina quickly. "You'll ruin my beautiful new sarong.

She pulled something somewhere and the sarong mysteriously became huge, like a sack, and slipped down easily from her waist to the floor. Van Es let his own sarong fall and the two formed a single heap on the floor just as Van Es and Justina soon formed a united couple on the bed.

Outside, the sky had grown dark and threatening. Soon, there were heavy claps of thunder and streaks of lightening. For a time, they lay resting in each other's arms, listening to torrential rain beating on the roof and hissing through the leaves of the trees in the little garden.

Justina asked slowly:

"Do you remember what you said to me last night?"

"No, I was too drunk," said Van Es.

"You said you loved me," she pressed.

"Sure. OK. I love you," he replied perfunctorily, as men do, to keep her happy. He knew very well what she wanted to hear.

"Do you mean it," Justina asked, as women do, doubting him even as he spoke.

"Ja. I mean it," said Van Es, tweaking her little nose playfully. "I really mean it."

That night, when it was time for Justina to go home and they parted, allowing the tips of their fingers to slip from each other's hands, Van Es caught her and pulled her back. She was fully dressed in her boots, her long dress, her high-necked blouse and her feathery hat but Van Es pulled her back, pulled her inside the house, pulled her back into the bedroom. There, on the bed, with her hat fallen off and her skirt round her waist, but otherwise still wearing everything, even her shoes, Van Es made love to her again and Justina made passionate love to Van Es.

"Let me stay," she whispered. "Let me stay!"

"Stay, stay," whispered Van Es hoarsely.

Next morning when he left at six, Justina remained at the villa. Another golden rule had been broken!

It was not a large house but Justina spent much of the day just wandering from room to room, running her fingers over the few pieces of European furniture, looking in cupboards, examining his things curiously, tidying up his uniforms and other clothes. Some of the clothes, and especially the socks, were so smelly that she gave a few pieces to Sup to give to the washerwoman. She did not attempt to clean because, even had the room been dusty, she wouldn't have noticed it. The primitive hut she shared with her family was always dusty but that was the reality of life in the kampong and nobody paid attention to it or noticed it.

At four o'clock, Van Es came home but today he did not sleep, except with Justina. But before six he said that she really must go home.

"Must I," she said sadly.

"Ja. You must. You cannot live here."

"But why not, if we are so happy together."

Van Es didn't want to expose his whole position to her, didn't want to explain the value he placed on his freedom, didn't want to tell her that he was not ready to give up the pleasure of the night, the delectable tasting of one little brown woman after another, didn't want to tell her the doubts he had about their relationship lasting, didn't want to explain to her how difficult it might be for him if his superiors found him in a relationship with a prostitute.

"And we'll be happy when we meet again," said Van Es firmly.

Justina realised that she could press him no further.

"I will see you at Atek's."

Again Justina demurred.

"Does it have to be Atek's?" Can we not just meet somewhere like a normal couple?"

Van Es was taken aback. She was right! They were behaving like a normal couple, not like a prostitute and a client. Sure, he gave her money but not in return for a specific favour; just money to help her, just a gift which seemed to flow as naturally from their relationship as giving her money to buy vegetables. Every man gave a woman money but it didn't always mean that he was paying for her 'services'. Van Es sighed.

"Where would you like to meet instead?"

"It's up to you," she replied irritatingly, with a happy smile.

Van Es thought furiously. He faced all the same problems as the ones he'd wrestled with when she wanted to go dancing! There were places where he just couldn't afford to be seen with her, like her though he did. She was the best sex partner he'd had recently. And she talked knowledgeably and sensibly, not chattering like a senseless bird or silent like a statue. Most importantly, she could communicate, because she spoke Dutch so well. There was no doubt about it, Justina was pretty, sensuous, clever and with a strong practical turn to her thinking that would make her a good wife for many - although not necessarily a senior officer in the

Netherlands Indies Army!

For her part, Justina did not go to Atek's because she liked the place. It was a means to an end, that was all. A place where she could earn money and a place where there was a chance she could catch a husband, just as her mother had done years ago. If it wasn't necessary to go to Atek's, Justina preferred not to. Going there pulled her back down to a social level from which she was trying hard to claw her way out, reminded her of a way of life she despised because respectable society despised it. Just as Van Es revelled in the sense of being secretly in a seductive and dangerous 'other world' of the ladies of the night, Justina revelled in the thought of escaping from it as soon as possible and living in a house like Van Es's as a respectable woman married to a fine, white, Dutch officer.

Van Es named a Chinese shop selling Dutch ice cream deserts in the Pasar Baru and agreed to meet her there next time.

Their relationship settled into a pattern in which they would meet on a Friday and Justina would stay at the villa until Monday. Actually, it was very convenient for Van Es because he could still visit the mess or the Club. Recently, he had become inexplicably bored with bridge at the Concordia, perhaps because it was so sedentary and passive. Instead he had taken up the much more active game of billiards, a game which somehow fitted better the upbeat mood of his relationship with Justina. Weeks passed like this until they ostensibly became very much a loving couple who, perhaps, really should have been married.

Justina genuinely liked Van Es. Behind Van Es's usual Dutch criticism of the Indies' lack of ethics and its inefficiencies, not to mention his penny pinching, he was a likeable man. He did not treat her badly, he always respected her, he never looked down on her for what she was, he had become her best friend - after Siti. Most importantly he was white, Dutch and, however low his lifestyle as a soldier, it had to be magnitudes better than her life in the native kampong.

Naturally, there were things she discussed with Siti which would not have been suitable for the ears of Van Es - her marriage hopes, for example! Even though Siti was her best friend she had not told her of her hope that Van Es would marry her. Siti would only have laughed scornfully and said something like:

"Fat chance of that!"

And, because she was part-Dutch her friends of her marriage hopes would just make them all think that she felt herself superior. On this subject Justina thought it best too keep quiet. Nothing excites jealousy in the Indies so much as someone else's success, and jealousy could be poisonously dangerous.

Justina was afraid that Van Es might tire of her. She wanted to catch him if she could. Married to a Dutch officer her miserable and humiliating life would be transformed, at least for a while, perhaps for ever. Even on days when she was feeling down, she tried always to be bright and cheerful in his presence and to wait on him hand and foot but she was conscious that her conversational abilities were limited because her life experience was limited. She started buying copies of the 'Batavia News'. She found most of its reading deadly boring but just by scanning the main headings, at least, she knew what was going on, knew what might interest a man like Van Es. The Major was pleased and soon began telling her about his day, exchanging little confidences with her and even asking her opinion. Like their physical relationship, their intellectual penetration of each other drew them closer and closer together.

They spent a lot of time at the villa but they also expanded the range of things they did together and places they went. On Saturday afternoons there was always a military band playing at the bandstand in the shady gardens of the Concordia and although Van Es couldn't take her there, they occasionally walked close by, beneath the trees, close enough to listen but far enough away not to be recognised. Van Es could not encourage her to go dancing but she liked it so much that he felt he had to think up diversions. Although it had been rather a long trip, once he had taken her for a day out near an old fishing village east of the Ancol, between the paddy fields and the Java Sea. It was a peaceful spot, thatched fishermen's huts sheltering beneath giant palms fringing the beach, long, thin outriggers drawn up on the shore. Europeans came here to picnic and even to swim in the ocean. From here you could see the old Dutch ship repair centre at Onrust Island as well as others in the Thousand Island chain. If you went too far east you came to the new harbour at Tanjung Priok but between Batavia and Tanjung Priok there were still many charming, unspoilt spots where it was even possible to be alone.

Justina had felt the long carriage drive bumpy, dusty and hot but her spirits returned after they had laid a picnic on the beach and eaten their fill. Their driver was just a speck in the distance and the rocky beach was otherwise quite deserted. It was truly beautiful on the sandy shore, the frilly edge of Justina's large sun-shade flapping gently above their heads, the sand white, the sea blue, cotton-wool clouds floating past. And there was a tremendous stillness there under the trees. They had set their picnic to one side of a giant tree which had been struck by lightening and left where it fell. Van Es was leaning on one elbow, looking down at Justina's contented little face, as she lie with her eyes closed. He kissed her softly on the lips. She kissed him back. They kissed more deeply and he lay partly across her. Van Es looked up and down the beach and, seeing no one, began pushing up her long dress to expose her legs and then her thighs.

"No," said Justina sharply, in alarm, trying to hold down her dress. "Hugo, please darling, not here."

"Here," Van Es insisted.

"Someone might come."

"No one will come. The beach is deserted."

"They will, they will, please don't."

If anyone comes I'll cover you with your dress."

Van Es kept pushing up the skirt with his strong hands as he kissed her and, the more passionately they kissed, the feebler her struggles became. Justina had her legs crossed under the long skirt but Van Es roughly pulled down her underwear and pushed her reluctant thighs apart.

"Hugo, please," she said again, feeling her total public exposure and trying vainly to close her legs. But Van Es was now between them and, over her protests, splayed her thighs wider as he mounted her so that the tops of her naked knees just showed above the fallen tree trunk.

Once she felt him, Justina gave in as completely as if she was in the privacy of their bedroom at the villa and loved him in a frenzy of lust that couldn't cease until each was gratified. And when it was:

"Oh, my love," she groaned, "Oh my love."

And so they loved and lived together in the most pleasurable way, Van Es even thinking less about his boring job and his prospects.

Van Es was happy for things to go on as they were but there was a constant pressure from Justina for him to clarify his intentions and make her ambiguous position clear. She had to push him but she could not afford to push him too fast or too far. She settled for a constant, good natured, sniping in which she would ask when they could really be seen in public together, when they could go together and sit under the trees outside the Concordia Club listening to the band like everyone else, when could they see a film together - she desperately wanted to see what a film was like, when could they go Saturday nights to the dances she loved so much, when could she join him openly at some of the wild parties she knew the military organised, in effect, when could their relationship be out in the open?

Van Es was well aware that Justina wanted to marry him and his thinking became poised on a knife edge. She was his now, She saw no other men. Despite the four-day gap in their relationship in the middle of the week, they were, to all intents and purposes, a couple, in a stable, long term, relationship which, perhaps because of Justina's profession, nevertheless still had plenty of exiting moments. She gave him wild sex, she entertained him, she looked after him, she was his friend. And, he agreed, it would have been nice for them to be able to go anywhere together instead of skulking around like fugitives on the fringes of events with him constantly worried about who might see them. But, marriage was a big step. Of course, he could marry her in the Indies and tough out the consequences but would he be brave - or foolish - enough to take her back to the Netherlands? And, while she seemed to give him everything he wanted, no Indies woman could possibly compare with a full blooded Hollander! What was the barracks saying: "Good in bed but not suitable for a wife!"

While he was agonising over these things and the relationship went on as before, one day his attention was held dramatically by a memorandum circulated in one of the numerous files which daily crossed his desk. It was headed ominously 'Officers Relationships With Native Women.' Van Es was so surprised he read it twice.

Basically, the memo sharply discouraged commissioned officers from having relationships with local girls and urged them, in the interests of racial purity and the growing colony of pure Dutch in the Indies, to cast their amorous attentions exclusively at the rapidly increasing numbers of Dutch women arriving in the East! To put it mildly, Van Es was thunderstruck. Based on this memo, Justina could mean the end of any prospect of promotion!

5

Tension rose quickly up Van Es's neck as he read the memo, like mercury in a heated thermometer. The circular was aimed squarely at people like him; 'Officers' it said in the title. The men were to be allowed to go on as before but officers were now expected to show racial loyalty! Since the Queen's Birthday Ball, when he had noticed more white women than ever at that female starved event, Van Es had sensed that the winds of change might soon be blowing more fiercely than hitherto against the custom of senior European officials living with indigenous women, even Eurasians. The minister's words at church had given a clear focus to this trend. And now came the memo from headquarters which left no doubt that the time was coming when, for senior officers, any but the most casual liaisons with local girls would be ruled out altogether, perhaps even these.

Because of the privilege of having his own villa, Van Es was in the enviable position of being able to entertain whatever women he chose - with no one the wiser, except his houseboy, Supadi, who thought the whole thing was a bit of a joke. Still, in the current climate of moral disapprobation, he was determined to be more careful than ever. The thought began to form in his mind that perhaps it was not wise to continue allowing Justina to stay at the villa every weekend. Van Es leant back in his wooden, service, chair. What really was his relationship with Justina? Did he really love her? Was a serious relationship possible? Could it be transplanted eventually to the Netherlands or was it doomed to die here in Batavia? And even if all the replies were positive, had he changed his mind about marriage - because this was what Justina obviously wanted? Was he ready to settle down or would he feel tied down in a way he had always dreaded? And if he was going to be tied down, wouldn't it be better with a Dutch woman who could love him as Justina did but whose friendship would inevitably be broader and deeper and who would not remain behind in the Indies when he went home? And what about children? Wouldn't it be better if these were Dutch children? Wouldn't the children be better off and guaranteed a proper place in society instead of always being somehow 'in between'. In Justina, he could see all the problems typical of the Eurasian - discomfort with Inlanders, a longing to be accepted into Dutch society and, as a result, really belonging to neither. If all these factors weren't enough, there was the vitally important matter of his promotion and what might happen to it if it became known now that he was more or less living with Justina!

As if to pile problems upon him, the black 'phone on his desk suddenly rang and the voice of Captain Janszen said:

"Good afternoon, Sir, Captain Janszen speaking."

Van Es sat bolt upright!

"Yes, Captain, what can I do for you?"

"It's about your appointment with Colonel Hogendorp, Sir."

Van Es's heart raced.

"Yes."

"The Colonel would like to see you in his office on Monday morning at around seven."

"Do you know what it's all about?"

"Sorry, Sir. No, Sir."

Van Es said he would be there, thanked him and replaced the receiver.

Had something been heard about Justina, was this to be a talk about promotion or was it something else? Van Es sat with his head in his hands wondering why his life had suddenly become so complicated! Worse still, tonight, Justina would be expecting him to meet her! Friday was the first night of their usual long weekend together. What could he say? What dare he say? How she he behave towards her with all this buzzing around in his head? Should he behave normally? Should he distance himself? Should he just stand her up! His in-tray was full but there was no way that he could concentrate on work. Van Es told the staff that he had a headache and went home to lie down to think on his bed at the villa.

Van Es quickly convinced himself that there was nothing to think about. Justina had to be dumped! He had been infatuated with her and their sex romps had been unforgettable but she expected too much, pushed too hard. He had never been convinced that he wanted to marry her or anyone else and the army memo had now made a marriage with a local woman utterly impossible. He knew that he was involved with Justina and wished heartily that he was not. If only he could return to the time when he had led his delicious 'secret' night life in Senen and at the villa with undemanding ladies who gave him what he wanted and went home! Despite the memo, perhaps he could still go back to living like that. The problem would be Justina. She would not give him up easily!

Then again, were it not for the new pressures from the military, he was in no hurry to give her up. He still liked her, they still had fun, they still talked and she still made love like a Java tigress! If only she wouldn't harp on and on about marriage and about having a normal relationship, just like any other couple. if only she would just behave like what she was, a prostitute!

On the other hand, there was no use pretending that their affair was as hot as it had been at the beginning. They had tasted each other over and over again. Nothing about their love-making was now a surprise, nothing was quite as exciting as it had been when they were discovering each other, feeling each other out, experimenting on each other, each showing the other every trick they knew to inflame torrid mutual passions. Of course, with familiarity and repetition, even the most ardent passions begin to cool and, as they saw more of each other, their lives together inevitably became more balanced and shared between many activities other than just sex. Even at the villa, Justina now spent more time cooking and generally looking after him than she did rolling about with him under the mosquito net. Their conversations could never get beyond the day-to-day - but, at least, there were conversations, and Van Es was still thankful for that. So, there were pros and cons....... Nevertheless, something would have to change! But what? And how? And with what consequences?

Van Es glanced sideways and saw the sarong she used when she stayed at the villa still slung over a chair back. He leant over to pull it to him and, smelling her perfume, he lay it over his nose and mouth, conjuring up her pale, beautiful image, and drinking in the smell and the memory of her. At that moment, he knew that he would see her as usual that night but, what might happen next, he had no idea!

With his mind tortured by fears and doubts, Van Es, dosed off into a restless sleep waking in time to dine at the mess before setting out to meet Justina at a place they had agreed — That night Justina looked more beautiful than ever. She was dressed for evening in a wide brimmed, flat, black hat with colourful but tasteful artificial flowers to one side, she was wearing a black tunic top and a crocheted white dress with the toes of black leather shoes poking out beneath. She had a penchant for black and white and truly looked as pretty as a picture. Above the black tunic was her pale face, framed in its cloud of thick black hair, her lips very red, her eyes deep black. And her perfume! Her perfume drugged him, as always. And, as always, a single touch of her soft, little hand inflamed him beyond reason. The more he thought about giving her up the more quickly he banished thoughts about their relationship going stale and the more inexorably he desired her. Justina was ecstatic that her lover seemed closer to her than ever and responded to him warmly.

Van Es had a strange premonition about this weekend. Despite all his positive feelings, he had a sense that this might actually be the last weekend that they would spend together! Knowing this made him even more ardent. Van Es had not seen her, or touched her, since Monday, so his lust was easily aroused. He suggested that, instead of going anywhere, they just went back to the villa, where, in his mind's eye, he could already visualise them naked and sweating, writhing together on the bed, as if they had never loved before.

"No more, no more, let me rest, please," Justina found herself gasping, night after searing night, until, Van Es, too, was exhausted and they both lay limp on the perspiration soaked sheets.

When Justina left on Monday there were black circles under her eyes and it took even longer than usual for their finger tips to finally slide apart at the door. Van Es always kept open the pair of long, French-doors, into the house from the veranda, but this morning, for some reason, he closed them firmly behind her and, for once, did not watch her slight figure walking away to board a waiting sado. The urgent thing in his mind was not Justina but the interview with Colonel Hogendorp at seven o'clock. He dressed promptly and with exemplary smartness and hurried to regimental headquarters by sado.

Hogendorp came straight to the point.

"It's about your application for a transfer," he said, clasping his hands on the empty desk top in front of him and looking Van Es full in the eyes.

"I am bound to say Major that I think it will be a waste for the army to encourage you to transfer to active duty. We have plenty of people who can fight but not so many who can do your job as well as you are doing it."

Van Es's face was a mask. He had at least expected a hearing. In his wilder flights of fancy he had even expected a transfer!

"No, Major," the Colonel went on soberly, like a headmaster correcting an errant pupil. "We cannot give you a transfer but we can give you more responsibility and try to make you work more interesting, perhaps even challenging."

The Colonel smiled encouragingly. Van Es remained passive. The only thing worse than the Ordnance Corps would be more work, he thought ungratefully.

"You don't look happy Major," said the Colonel, with the hint of a smile. "But perhaps it will cheer you up if I tell you that we are thinking of promoting you to full Colonel."

Van Es's jaw dropped. His brain raced. First he was being double promoted; second such a promotion carried massive implications for the size of unit to which he would be attached, and, third, it must mean a completely different line of work.

"You're thinking it might mean a new job," the Colonel said, apparently reading his mind. "No such luck I'm afraid. As I've told you, we value your skills where they are. You would be a difficult man to replace."

Van Es hardly followed. Was he to be promoted to colonel merely to continue doing what he hated doing?

"Let me explain. You are a regimental officer but several regiments need your talents so we would like to find a way of spreading you around, using you as a co-ordinator, if you will."

"Sir?"

"What we have in mind is to create for you a new staff post at brigade level from which you would manage, co-ordinate and monitor the supplies of all headquarters units."

"That's a big job," said Van Es involuntarily.

"We think you are the man to do it," said the Colonel seriously. 'It is a big job but it's a job that needs doing badly. We are convinced that over-payment, mismanagement and outright waste are costing us a fortune."

Van Es smiled. he could not remain cold and inscrutable in the face of such an offer.

"It is a great honour, Sir," he managed to say.

His mind raced along, reviewing the possibilities. True, he had wanted both fame and fortune and had thought fame more likely to be achieved on the battlefield. But wasn't being made a staff Colonel fame? Was this not a giant step also along the road to riches?

"You are not disappointed, Major."

"I don't know what to say, Sir. It's all very unexpected."

"And you'll accept."

"Of course, Sir, Thank you, Sir."

"Don't thank me too much, Major. You have earned this, otherwise we would not have given it to you. One other thing. Even before the matter of your promotion cropped up the army had decided to award you a distinguished service medal. The presentation will be at next Saturday's awards ceremony at Koningsplein."

Van Es could not restrain a gasp! He had thought that he was a back-room boy that nobody noticed yet he was about to receive his first medal - without ever being in a single battle!

The military is not all about fighting, Major," the Colonel went on. "Of course, as the ultimate power in the Indies, we must be in a position to win. But for our front line troops to win they need the support of dedicated and effective supply units in the rear."

"I appreciate that, Sir. I just thought that I might do better at something else."

"You might Van Es, you might," said the Colonel. But we value you where you are as much as if you were at the front line - not where you are," he corrected, "what you do, because once this promotion is effective you'll be moving to a new office at headquarters."

As was so usual in his life, Van Es was of two minds. The promotion was not the future he'd hoped for but it was still a very handsome future. He could already see himself in a Colonel's uniform enjoying a Colonel's respect and Colonel's privileges!

"I'm very grateful, Sir," he said.

"You have nothing to be grateful for," said the Colonel rising to escort Van Es to the door. As I said before, whatever you are receiving you have earned."

They paused at the door.

"You're not married, are you Van Es?"

"Not yet, Sir."

"Find yourself a nice Dutch woman, Major. There are plenty coming out now. It's always better for senior officers to be safely married to one of our own!"

Van Es swallowed hard. The Colonel chuckled and patted him on the back.

"If all goes well, we'll be meeting again at Koningsplein next week."

Van Es's mind was in turmoil! He was to be made a staff officer! Promoted to full colonel! But what if they found out about Justina? Would everything gained then slip from his grasp. And hadn't he been warned, not only in the Memo but, directly, by the Colonel when he had slapped him cordially on the back and encouraged him to take a Dutch wife!

Van Es walked briskly back to his office, as befitted a man who now bore the responsibilities of a colonel. He immersed himself in his work that day with more vigour and more attention to detail than ever. The outer office staff knew he had been to see the Colonel and wondered what had transpired as he yelled first for this one and then for that and kept them coming and going with a succession of files and documents. Everyone breathed a sigh of relief when four o'clock came and they heard him calling out that he was going home, followed shortly by the grating of his key in the lock.

Van Es had more or less decided not to say anything to anyone about his good fortune until his promotion was formally listed - although, in his heart, he doubted he could avoid telling brother officers at the mess that night. Actually, the prospects were suddenly so bright that he was positively dying to tell someone his good news and, if he could have trusted her, would have rushed immediately to tell Justina. He knew that she would be as delighted as he was. After all, she, too, was ambitious. Van Es was soon relaxing in his usual position on his bed at the villa, his arms behind his head, smoking thoughtfully. It was not just a question of whether he should or should not tell Justina. What was at stake today was the future of their relationship! Everything had to be reviewed before he saw her again! Everything, he thought, could be resolved into two basic questions: Had the relationship between himself and Justina any long term future? How might an enduring relationship affect his promotion?

Van Es could see instantly that, however much he liked Justina, there could never be any question now of his actually marrying her! If he took a small risk by visiting her in Senen, if she never stayed at the villa again, if they never went out in public again, it was just possible that the relationship could continue, albeit narrowed down to basic sex at Atek's! But would a woman who had been as close to him as Justina accept that? Would a woman hoping for marriage accept that? Van Es had come to know the pride of Justina and, without asking, he knew that she would never accept the humiliation of being relegated to her previous role as a mere prostitute, serving his needs in a filthy back-room at Atek's.

The sarong Justina always wore when at the villa was still draped in its familiar place over the chair-back. Van Es looked at it and thought about all the good times they had had together since they had first met - about their wanton love making, about her youthful energy and constant enthusiasm, about their crazy, exuberant, dancing, about how happy she had always been in his company, about the special Indies ways she had shown him, about the way she had made his meals and looked after him, about her common sense, her infectious humour, about her adoring eyes, her willingness to please, her soft body, her loving embrace! What more could a man possibly want! But he gave the answer himself, in a word - promotion!

Van Es could not see himself with a Dutch wife after his many liaisons with Indies girls whose succulence would never be known by those who had not tasted them. Yet, he could not afford to risk his relationship with Justina ruining the career for which he had forsaken Holland, for which he had come to the Indies in the first place and for the success of which he thirsted as much, if not more, than he longed for Justina. Who knew? Perhaps she would agree to keep seeing him at Atek's only. In a sense, that would be an ideal solution. He would have to sacrifice the wider aspects of the relationship but, at least, they could still enjoy sex together. If she would not agree to continue seeing him under the new circumstances, there were plenty of other girls around whom he could safely meet for an hour or two while keeping at a safe distance!

There was no doubt about it. The relationship with Justina would have to be returned to the simple level of sex for cash. If Justina would not accept that, it would have to be broken off! If it came to this, he would suffer the short term affects of withdrawal from what had become a cosy relationship and she would probably be disappointed and angry. But his promotion would be safe. As to looking for a Dutch wife, such a horror could await the outcome of events. Who knew yet with what vigour the new policy of forbidding native women to officers would actually be enforced?

He did not see Justina again until Friday, which was a blessing, because it enabled him to consciously and deliberately block her out from his mind and to grow accustomed to the idea of not having her around, perhaps even of not seeing her! When Friday came, of course, he had a choice. He could simply not turn up at their meeting place or he could do so as planned and tell her all about the promotion - but not probability that he might have to see less of her and the certainty that she could never again stay at the villa! In the event, he decided on the latter course and used the excuse of Saturday's presentation to avoid inviting her to the villa as usual on Friday night. As he'd expected, Justina was ecstatic about his good fortune. She flung her arms round his neck with a beaming smile and kissed him passionately. That night, they walked slowly beneath the dark trees of Weltevreden, holding hands as lovers like to do and talking of this and that and, at a particular moment, he went his way and she went hers.

Next day, Van Es was too busy to try to spot her face in the crowd at Koningsplein. In any case, the field was so enormous it was virtually impossible. He had given her permission to come and watch, provided she made no attempt to approach him or obtain his acknowledgement. When he walked forward to receive his new stars that day from General Van des Velden, Van Es was bursting with pride. As he marched, his booted feet crashed down on the ground with a sound like thunder, his sword was held tightly at a perfect vertical, his uniform was impeccable. This was achievement! This was glory! This was what Van Es had yearned for as long as he could remember! The stars were pinned on, and, then his medal, stars, medal, buttons, weapons all glinting in the bright morning sun. The General congratulated him. Van Es saluted. Bands played. Regiments marched past. Van Es could feel the irresistible power of the Netherlands colonial government in his very blood and bones! And with his new stars he could feel his own growing power! Sense his own ability to influence and decide, sense a destiny at one with the forces he served with unswerving loyalty!

Justina saw him walk forward to receive his promotion and decoration, watched him parade proudly and she was deeply happy. Van Es was her man. His success was her success. She was bursting with excitement and had no idea how she was going to wait until the evening to see him. She was puzzled why she couldn't have gone to the villa after the parade but Van Es seemed to have some good reasons and she had resigned herself to having to wait. How she would love him tonight, her colonel! "Colonel Van Es," she practised to herself. "Colonel and Mrs Van Es!" She had wanted to meet him as usual at their favourite ice cream parlour, but Van Es had said that he would be late and that Atek's was closer so he hoped she wouldn't mind meeting there, just this once. Justina did mind. She minded very much, actually, because to meet at Atek's was a like a going back to something she had thought was behind her, a return to a way of life she hoped, with all her mind and body, was over, a stark, unpleasant reminder of her real place in Batavian society. But she suspected nothing. Their relationship seemed as it had ever been. Last weekend at the villa had even been better than it had ever been! She couldn't stop herself going to Atek's early in the hope that Van Es would come early too, and that they could be together sooner. There were so many things to discuss!

While she waited she told Siti what had happened and about her hopes.

"I really hope it all works out as you'd like," said Sitidoubtfully. "You know, not many girls from here get to marry senior Dutch officers. If it really happens it will be a miracle."

"I believe in miracles," said Justina with a smile.

Siti smiled weakly.

'If he doesn't marry you, you'll be very disappointed," she said with concern.

"You don't know how much he adores me," smiled Justina triumphantly. 'No man has ever loved me as he has. And, don't forget that I'm virtually living with him."

"But has he asked you to marry him?"

"No. But I'm sure he will. Maybe tonight. He told me he has something important to say to me."

"You can never tell with men," said Siti, who had certainly known more than her fair share of them. "It depends whether he loves you for yourself or just for sex."

"He loves me," said Justina confidently. I know he loves me. We are best friends even."

Van Es was late, but, eventually, Justina saw his familiar, tall, form in the doorway, looking around, trying to find her. Spotting her, he came across right away. For once, Justina could smell that he had not been drinking at the mess.

"Let's go out into the garden at the back," Van Es suggested, taking her arm and steering her that way. "I want to talk to you."

There was no place to sit in the little garden, bordered by thick bamboos, but there was no one there and it was private, accept when the odd person went to the outside lavatory. Van Es had not kissed her and looked serious as he paced up and down in the limited space, encouraging her to walk by his side. Justina tried to hold him but he brushed her hand away.

"Dutch officers have been forbidden to have native women partners," he said suddenly, brutally pinpointing the only real issue between them.

Justina was aghast. She stopped walking and stared at him with dropped jaw and wide, serious eyes. She was an intelligent woman and she immediately saw the implication.

"But I am not a native woman," she said with a haughty toss of her head.

"You are in the eyes of the Dutch," said Van Es flatly.

Justina swallowed hard. She did not touch his arm affectionately as she would normally have done but gripped his arm firmly, forcing him to stop and look at her.

"What are you trying to say," she asked with a mixture of fear and anger in her voice. "You said you had something to tell me. Tell me now."

Van Es drew back from her, his tense manner and his government uniform putting a distance between them that had not been there before.

"If we go on seeing each other as we have been, I could lose my promotion," he said very deliberately, looking at her full in the eyes.

Justina stared at him. She could hardly believe her ears. She didn't know what to say. She didn't want to say anything. Didn't want him to say anything. She just wanted the whole conversation to stop right there. But Van Es started speaking again and his words were like nails hammered into her brain.

"We can still see each other, if you wish, here at Atek's, but you cannot stay at the villa again."

"And we can never marry," Justina finally managed to gasp.

"We can never marry," confirmed Van Es, with emphatic finality.

Justina walked round and round in small circles in front of him while Van Es looked on, waiting for her to speak. He could see that a great burden now lay upon her, a great tragedy had overtaken her. She stopped in front of him, looking searchingly up at him, trying to divine from his face whether there was still the smallest hope.

"We are so happy together," she said tearfully, bowing her head in grief. 'You love me, I know you love me."

Justina sobbed uncontrollably. Van Es moved to take her in his arms but then drew back, leaving her to face her pain all by herself.

"We can still see each other," he said weakly.

Justina quickly dried her eyes and lifted her wet face to his. Gone was the initial surprise, gone was the tearful disappointment. Now she was angry! Her face, beautiful when it smiled, now assumed a demeanour that Van Es had never seen before. All that was black in it overwhelmed everything that was white. Her eyes blazed so terrifyingly that Van Es, the soldier, took a step back. She was so upset that she had actually become ugly and frightening. If there was such a thing as black magic, Van Es thought, here, surely, was one of its witches!

"You promised to marry me," Justina almost shouted in a storm of intense hurt, rejection, frustration and anger.

"No. I did not," Van Es answered firmly. "I told you that I loved you."

"It's the same thing."

"Not at all. Every man tells a woman that."

"So, you didn't mean any of it."

Van Es felt embarrassed and cornered.

"I meant what I said. But I never said that I would marry you. That's what *you* said."

Justina suddenly switched from the Dutch side of her personality to her Indies side.

"You Dutch are all so tricky," she almost spat at him.

"*I'm* not being tricky," said Van Es in self defence. "A new regulation has been made and I must obey it, or suffer the consequences."

"I suppose now you'll take a Dutch wife," Justina almost sneered.

"*If* I marry, it will have to be to a Dutch wife."

Justina now switched back to the European side of her make-up.

"I have Dutch blood in my veins," she shouted angrily. I'm as good as any Dutch wife, better in fact."

"But you are not Dutch."

"Every day, more and more Dutch come here, driving us out. You Dutch created us with your lusts and now you want to treat us like Inlanders. But I am not an Inlander," she shrieked, "I am Dutch."

Van Es turned to leave. He could see there was no point in even trying to talk to her. She was distraught with rage. She caught his arm and used all her strength to spin him round.

Wounded to the very core of her being, she screamed insultingly: "You Dutch are all full of shit."

Van Es stiffened instantly. Any passivity he may have felt left him immediately. He hated the contorted face he saw before him but most of all he detested Justina for her spiteful and obviously heartfelt attack on his people. In a flash he congratulated himself on not marrying her! It was clear now that behind her affected adoration was a burning hatred! A big and powerful man with a hot temper, Van Es instinctively shot out his arm and gripped her little throat above her high collar, forcing her backwards.

"Don't say those things to me," he hissed, his hand tight on her throat. "Never speak to me like that. In fact, never speak to me at all. Do you understand! I don't want to see your ugly face ever again. If I come here, be sure you are not here. Is that clear?"

Van Es's anger was now also out of control. Justina stared at him with eyes bulging and, realising the danger in what he was doing, Van Es quickly dropped his hand and curbed his temper. Behind the bamboos Siti stopped herself from rushing to Justina's rescue.

Justina stood sobbing uncontrollably, her face even uglier as it contorted with pain. What woman's face is beautiful when she cries? Van Es shuddered and made to leave again. He felt rather than saw Justina fling her arms round his legs to prevent him walking and despised her as he looked down at her grovelling at his feet, her clothes smeared with dirt, her hair a mess, her face streaked with tears and make-up.

"Hugo," she choked, "I beg of you, please, please marry me." She added very softly after a slight pause, "I'm pregnant."

It was now Van Es's turn to be flabbergasted.

"Pregnant," he said with undisguised disbelief. "Is this some trick."

"I swear," she sobbed. "It's not a trick. I haven't had my period. We're going to have a child."

"You're going to have a child, not me," said Van Es coldly, watching her scramble up. "Why didn't you take some precautions."

Justina laughed hysterically. "Precautions! What precautions! How could I take precautions with you getting into me four times a night!"

Van Es was silent.

"It's your child," she said simply, and, then, almost in a whisper, "It's your child."

Van Es appeared to think for a moment while Justina kept her head lowered at his feet.

" How do I know that," he snapped suddenly and cruelly.

Justina leapt up with all her strength and hit him in the face as hard as a smaller person could, spinning herself off balance and drawing blood from his mouth.

"That's how you know it," she hissed.

"That finishes it," roared Van Es, wiping the bright red blood onto the white sleeve of his uniform.

Justina stood quietly now, with a quietness that was at once as resigned as it was deadly.

"It won't be finished until you marry me," she said slowly and definitely.

"I will never marry you," said Van Es.

"Not even if I tell your precious General what you've done."

"Don't do that," Van Es hissed back at her dangerously, again going up close to her so that she could feel his hot breath on her face. Don't ever think of doing that," he repeated menacingly, "or you'll be very, very sorry indeed."

Van Es turned and strode out of the garden. Justina fell to her knees with her head in her hands. Siti rushed forward to kneel beside her and hold her head in her tender arms.

6

Van Es remained in a raging temper all the way home - in a temper with Justina for thinking she could trap him into marriage and in a temper with himself for loving someone he had been brought to think of as an ugly, loud mouthed, whore! He could see now that all her sweetness had been fake! Marriage had been her sole objective from the beginning, even if it was to someone whose land and culture she obviously hated! Van Es would never forget her black and twisted face! Her venom against the Dutch! Her hatred! He banged his fist on the back of the leather seat of the sado he had hired and shook the metal pole holding up the flimsy covering, designed to act as a sun shade during the heat of the day. The driver knew his passenger was angry and, he feared, drunk so he ignored the events behind him and drove stoically. A drunk Dutchman could be danger indeed! Better to stay quiet and do nothing to attract his attention.

Van Es slammed into the villa, throwing boots and clothes everywhere, and lay down on his bed with his arms over his head. He wasn't even slightly tired as, again and again he turned Justina's incredible behaviour over in his mind. Seeing her familiar sarong on its usual chair-back he jumped up, grabbed it, and threw it off the back veranda towards Sup's quarters. In the morning, he would tell him to burn it! Van Es wanted nothing in the house to remind him of that appalling woman. He returned to the bed, banging his fists on his forehead in unstilled rage at what Justina had said to him, at her insults, at her threats!

Van Es's first reaction was that since she was a prostitute, a nobody, a woman of absolutely no account, no one in the Dutch military would listen to her. Even if they listened it was extremely unlikely that they would believe her or side with her against one of their own. Van Es smiled cruelly to himself. He was safe! There was nothing she could do which could harm him! Then again, she was part Dutch. She could speak Dutch. She had had a rudimentary education. From what he knew of her, she would not be anywhere near as terrified as pure natives to approach Dutch uniformed officials. And, since she hadn't always seemed ugly and repulsive to him, there was every reason to suppose that, on slight acquaintance, others would find her attractive, too.

"The bitch," he said to himself, clenching and unclenching his fists at his side. "I wish I had never met her."

Justina sat in the dirt behind Atek's for a long time before moving, her tear-stained face in Siti's dress.

"I'll take you home," said Siti caringly, wiping her face dry and clean on the hem of her long dress.

Justina was still sobbing quietly, but, very slowly she lifted her head to look at Siti, her eyes mirroring the unspeakable agony of her heart and soul.

"Why?" Siti, she groaned in anguish. "Why did he do it? Why was he so Siti

Siti sat close to her and stroked her dishevelled hair.

"He's gone now," she said softly, observing the obvious as Inlanders were wont to do. "Forget him," she added with a woman's certainty. "If he hurts you once he will hurt you again."

Eventually, Justina was calm. She smoothed her clothes, repaired her appearance as best she could and walked erect and proud with Siti through the garden to a sado which took them both to Justina's kampong home. Her family had been asleep for hours, as was the native tradition. Siti wanted to stay with her friend and the two of them removed their 'uniform' clothes, put on sarongs and curled up, side by side, on sleeping mats on the hard floor, Justina falling quickly into a healing sleep, with her head in the crook of Siti's arm.

Next day, Van Es went to church as usual. His first act on waking, had been to order Sup to burn Justina's sarong. Then he had banished her from his mind as absolutely as if she had never existed. He felt good this morning, felt powerful within his new rank of Colonel, felt respected. Around him were the respectable upper classes of Batavia, dressed in their Sunday best, a far cry from the squalid scene at Atek's, with its squalid whore that he had walked out on last night. This was the life for him! The life of a powerful, upper class Tuan besar! If he played his cards right, nothing could hold him back now!

Van Es joined in the service with gusto, saying all the prayers, loudly singing all the hymns. The Minister's theme this week was once again for respectable Dutch people to avoid becoming tainted with the unwholesome beliefs and ways of the Inlanders, to stick to their own! Van Es had no difficulty agreeing. Suppose he had married Justina? To what backward beliefs and habits would she have exposed him? Would he eventually have been dragged down to her level, living as a few renegade whites did, in the hovel-lined alleys of the kampong with his black mistress? How indescribably black she had looked last night? And what hatred she had had! Would she have secretly hated him even after they had married? Would even his life have been safe? Might not the day have come when she resorted to the black arts of her people and tried to kill him! Van Es congratulated himself. He was well rid of her!

Justina, meanwhile, was a centre of attention. Her mother had taken Siti's place, rocking her gently in her lap, her sad-faced sisters patted her head and caressed her until, drenched in love, she was allowed to wash and dress and her old grandmother fed her some tid bits of food from a bowl - "to keep up her strength."

As her family petted her and looked after her, Justina looked around with her beautiful, but now dull and sad, eyes. She was grateful for the tender kindness, but it was a defeat for her to be comforted by her family like this. When Van Es had choked her with his hand last night, he had choked and killed her hopes! When he had cut off their relationship, he had cut off her future! He had condemned her to live again the life of a kampong girl! But a kampong girl who could never be part of an Inlander kampong while the Dutch blood in her veins forced her to think and act differently to the people around her, even her own family, while her Dutch blood gave her no rest from the struggle to escape from life in the poverty stricken hut of an Inlander family to try to take her 'natural' position as a member of the Dutch community.

Justina was not a quitter. In any case, she really was pregnant. Steps had to be thought out. Actions taken. She had never before seen Van Es as he had been last night, his face red and twisted with so much rage and hatred that she thought he was going to kill her! She had not known that he had such a temper because he had always been loving and kind. Had she married him, maybe he would really have killed her! Justina immediately stopped herself from thinking such terrible thoughts. She thought she knew that Van Es was not an evil man. Certainly, he could never bring himself to kill her!

After all, he had loved her and she had loved him; they had been as sweet and tender together as it was possible for a man and woman to be - with never a hint of a black mood, or of violence. Last night, Van Es had been upset. She understood that he was afraid to lose his promotion. He was not a complex man. What soldiers were? In the circumstances, he had done what he thought he had to do! Justina managed a faint smile. He had even offered to continue the relationship so long as they could meet at Atek's. But he had hurt her deeply. Made her say things which, perhaps, she shouldn't have said! It was Sunday. He would be at home this afternoon. She would go to him. She would tell him that she understood. Try to make him see her point of view. She would even apologise for any intemperate things she may have said.

Her family were horrified when she told them her plan.

"Don't go. Don't go," her mother said, wide-eyed with fear and horror. "He is a soldier. He may kill you."

When Van Es returned to the villa from his Sunday rijstavel at the mess, Justina rose from his favourite wicker chair where she had been waiting with her back to the path. Concealed by the chair-back Van Es had not seen her as he approached.

"Hugo," she said tenderly, holding out both hands to him and smiling tenderly.

"You," exploded Van Es in an instant uncontrollable rage. "You dare to come to my house and sit in my chair.

Justina tried to speak.

"Hugo, I......."

"Get out, Get out," Van Es screamed, pushing her so roughly off the high veranda that she slipped and fell, cutting one knee badly on the sharp wooden edge.

Van Es followed, dragged her up and forced her, limping, along the path to the public road. Tears streamed down her face as he pushed her roughly into the dust, almost under the hooves and wheels of a passing sado.

"Never come here again," Van Es roared hoarsely. "If you come again, I'll set the police on you!"

Hatred welled up in Justina as it had last night. She had come to the Villa with her heart still brimming with love, with the hope that their 'misunderstandings' could be cleared up, with the hope that they could still share a life together. Van Es's response had been to throw her into the gutter! Not even a dog deserved to be treated like that!

Justina brushed off her clothes, picked up her fallen hat and limped off along the road before taking a sado home. The cut on her leg stung unbearably, a throbbing reminder of Van Es's cruelty. Now she was not sure if she really loved him any more. What woman would want to love such a beast? But she was pregnant! She was trapped! She would soon be having a child to drag on her all day, that would have to be looked after every hour, that would plunge her deeper into poverty, that would destroy her prime asset, her figure, a child that, at least for a while, would prevent her from using even her body to earn and income and to try to secure a brighter future.

The child she was carrying belonged to Van Es, and he should marry her! What husband could she hope to get if she already had one child?

Without further thought, she knew that she would write to him, that she would make one last try to explain everything, to convince him, to try to get him to meet her, to try to bind him to her again with love. Filled with her mission, she went home to write. Their's was not a house in which one would normally find writing materials but Justina prided herself on her ability, alone in the family, to write, and she always kept a little stock of paper by her for notes and such like. She wrote for a long time in her neat, woman's hand-writing and, that night, asked her loyal friend Siti to carry the note to Van Es. After that she could only wait.

How much more hurt she would have been if she could have seen that, on recognising who the note was from, Van Es threw it away unread! Which was a pity, because, in conclusion, Justina had said that if she did not hear from him she would have no option but to place the whole matter before General Van des Velden with a view to securing a fair hearing and winning a just outcome. She apologised for troubling such a great and busy man but said that she was desperate and had nowhere else to turn. In conclusion, she said that, if the General ignored her, she would have no option but to wait outside his office every day until he heard her case!

Van Es was therefore taken completely by surprise to be summoned to the General's office.

Van des Velden was apoplectic.

"This is exactly the kind of thing we most want

Dutch officers to avoid," he stormed.

"You've got to do something about this woman, Colonel Van Es. Otherwise she's going to bring discredit not only on you but on the army and on the entire Netherlands Indies colonial service."

Van Es returned to his office seething with anger. Too many things were happening to him too fast. As he stepped back into his familiar office, boys were removing the last of his things to a new office further along the road linking Senen to Meester Cornelis, where his new headquarters unit was based and where a new office awaited him with the words 'Colonel H. Van Es' inscribed proudly and boldly on the door. Even as he moved to take up his new life, to begin an important new step on the ladder to fame and fortune, he was being threatened with discredit and, worse still, his General was being threatened with discredit. And, not only the two of them but the entire army and the whole service! Van Es ground his teeth. He would never marry that black bitch! But he would find a way to stop her mouth once and for all! She had been warned!

Van Es guessed that if there was one man who could stop her it would be Atek. Atek ran girls and although Van Es didn't know whether Justina was one of his women, the mere fact that Justina operated from Atek's should give the brothel operator some control over her. He knew instinctively that his next step was to speak to Atek but he didn't want to turn up at the brothel and run slap into Justina! But would he? It was still early in the week and Van Es couldn't remember ever seeing her there until Thursday or Friday. He decided to go that night. It was a small risk if he could talk to Atek and get things over with.

His intuition had been right. Justina was not there and, more importantly, Atek and his henchmen were squatting outside in their usual place so it was easy for Van Es to invite them to talk in the back garden where he had last quarrelled with Justina and, of course, where no one would see them. Once Atek understood what Van Es wanted he invited him to step into the privacy of a small shack standing by itself at the rear of the bamboo garden and which he evidently used as a storeroom.

Atek smiled evilly when he heard what Van Es wanted.

"I don't care what you do but I want the bitch shut up forever," Van Es had said.

"Forever?" Tuan, Atek had queried, to be sure he fully understood. "Justina is not a woman easily frightened. And she is stubborn. We might have to do more than frighten her."

"Do whatever has to be done. Only do it quickly before she ruins my whole life!"

Atek was a wily businessman. He did nothing for nothing! Drinks were brought and they haggled over the cost of whatever it was Atek would do to "shut up Justina forever." A sum was agreed and Van Es promised to return the following night with half the fee in cash - the other half to be paid when the punishment had been inflicted and Justina's silence guaranteed.

"You must tell no one about this Atek," Van Es warned.

"Nor you, Colonel," Atek said menacingly.

Their bond of silence sealed, Van Es left Justina's fate in Atek's hands and went to work next day feeling less apprehensive. He felt a dark, depressing cloud was about to be swept away from his life, a nagging threat about to be removed. He hoped only that Atek would act to deter Justina before Justina carried out her threat to camp out outside the General's office. For the next day or two, while striving abnormally hard to be calm, cheerful and optimistic, Van Es jumped with fright every time his telephone rang, in case it was General Van des Velden!

Atek needed time to make his plan and lay his trap for Justina. The most obvious course, he thought, was to make Justina believe that Van Es wanted to see her. Atek couldn't write so a message had to be sent by a boy, with all the many possibilities of the boy getting it wrong! Nevertheless, there was no other way, and a reliable boy was identified, rehearsed and dispatched to Justina's. He told the, at first bewildered, but rapidly ecstatic, woman that Van Es couldn't meet her openly but wanted to see her to patch things up. He would be waiting in a sado, tonight, in the dark, under the trees lining the road between Weltevreden and Senen. Justina would recognise the sado because it would have no sun roof or cover. If she, came by sado, she should dismiss her driver after leaving Senen and walk the short distance along the road to the waiting sado beneath the trees. In this way secrecy would be guaranteed!

There was nowhere in the little house where

she could be alone but Justina wished so much that she could have been. She would have rushed to a mirror just to see for herself how happy she was! But there was no mirror and her rapture had to be kept deep within herself, reflected only in a tiny smile playing about the corners of her mouth.

"Don't go alone," her mother pleaded. "These belandas are capable of anything. "You don't know what he might do.

Justina smiled.

"Ma," she said. It's all right. I know him. He's a good man, really. He was just upset. I'm sure he doesn't mean to harm me."

The old mother sat on he floor, rocking herself gently too and fro, her eyes agonised with anxiety. Her sisters watched silently as she made her preparations.

Justina spent a long time in the mandi, washing herself thoroughly, and she emerged with a towel round her waist and another like a turban over her wet hair. She dried herself quickly and lay down, while her grandmother rubbed skin-moistening, sweet smelling oil all over her supple young body.

"You always had a beautiful body," said her grandmother admiringly. "It's a pity you've cut your lcg."

Justina dressed simply. She felt that simple things made the most stunning impact and she selected clothes which flattered her natural beauty. She didn't have many European clothes but, since tonight might be the most important in her entire life, she chose with special care. The blouse was white but frilly with a collar like a fairy's ruff. Her long dress was jet black with deep pleats at front and back and with a high, wide waist. Her flat, wide brimmed hat was also black with the usual bright, feathery, spray to one side. Justina applied copious quantities of the perfume she knew drove Van Es wild - behind her ears, on her throat, her neck, between her breasts.

The older, traditional, women in the room screwed up their noses.

At last she was ready and stood before them on the verge of what could be the greatest triumph of her life.

"Please, please, don't go. We beg you," her mother and grandmother pleaded again and again.

"When I come back, hopefully, it will be to tell you all that I'm going to be married," Justina said with a bright and brace smile. Her eyes looked a little tired but there was more than a trace of the old sparkle in them tonight.

Justina was young, confident, Dutch and a woman of the world. Her mother and grandmother were but kampong women who understand nothing. Her sisters were too young to have any worthwhile experience.

Tonight, she was the old Justina again, confident, optimistic, off to meet her Dutch lover, the white man who would marry her and take her away from the squalor and shame of life in the kampong!

She hired a delman, so that she could see better, and peered excitedly into the gloom to try make out the coverless sado she had been told to look out for. Eventually, she saw it parked under the trees, a little distance from the road. Justina positively leapt from the delman. She wanted to look her radiant best for Van Es and forced herself not to hurry too much nor to limp, even though her leg still hurt.

There was no one in the sado but Justina could make out a figure in a crumpled white suit standing under a big tree with his back to her. Fleetingly, she wondered why Hugo was not on the look out for her, was not as excited to see her as she was to see him. Enthusiasm overcame caution and she ran forward eagerly.

"Hugo, Hugo, it's me," she called happily.

The figure in the crumpled white suit did not move. When she was right up to him the man slowly turned and she found herself staring into the black face and menacing eyes of Atek!

Too late, Justina tried to check her head-long rush and draw back, but Atek had sprung at her and dragged her unceremoniously to him by the frilly front of her white blouse, ripping off some of the buttons. Justina opened her mouth to shout for help but immediately a foul smelling rag was forced between her silky lips, staining them red with blood. She sensed Atek's two henchmen leap up from where they had been squatting in the dark. Strange hands seemed to be everywhere, grabbing at her, tearing her clothes, pushing her, pulling her. She tried to fend them off but two hands were no match for six! Everything happened very fast. She felt her hands seized and the three strong men hustle her away from the road, out of sight among the impenetrable, concealing trees. Any one of the men was a head taller than Justina and twice as broad! If they were going to hurt her there was no doubt that they could do it terribly! Justina's heart raced and skipped beats, she was so afraid. She was breathless, but because of the rag in her mouth she couldn't get enough air. She thought she was going to die of fear and tension.

The three men forced her to the ground and she was in no doubt what for! Something the likes of them would never have had from her even for money! She writhed and squirmed like a tigress, drawing upon every ounce of energy but a henchman had hold of each arm and Atek threw his whole weight on her once she was on her back in the dirt. She tried to knee him, to kick him, to hurt him - anything to make him leave her alone. In her frenzy she managed to pull free one of her arms. But the freedom was too short to achieve anything! Atek immediately punished her by hitting her full in the face with his closed fist and pummelling her head with his open palm, smashing some of her even, white, teeth and bruising the pale skin of her face. Justina's eyes were wide with terror.

One man now had hold of both of her arms and pulled them tightly above her head with his bare feet pressing down on her shoulders. Atek and his helper concentrated on catching hold of Justina's violently kicking legs and, once accomplished, Atek dropped down astride her, ripping open her blood-stained blouse and coarsely fondling her milk white breasts. As Van Es had used to do, he didn't bother to try to take off her long dress but just pulled it up roughly around her waist. Tearing off her pretty underwear his big, dirty fingers plunged between her legs, poking into her like iron rods. The pain underneath her was savage, her arms hurt unbearably, her mouth was full of blood, which she was forced to either swallow or choke on. Atek pushed aside her unheld thigh so that he could get between her legs. He forced himself into her so that the new pain of involuntary penetration forced tears from her beautiful eyes.

Justina had been handled by plenty of men. This wasn't the first time her private parts had been exposed. But always she was handled admiringly and with soft, adoring, caresses. Now her body was being ripped and torn by a stinking brute of a man who did it as if it no longer had feelings. Atek grunted and groaned bestially as he took her, his big hands tightly gripping her tiny waist to be sure that she could not move and took the full force of his thrusts. She could hear his two henchman making crude and disgusting comments and she knew what was coming next. Inflamed by watching his pleasure, the henchmen urged him to hurry up and finish.

Justina was given no chance to close her legs before another man was between them. When Atek rose, another stinking, sweating man fell on top of her, lunging into her. Then the second man rose and the third man, now mad with lust because of what he had seen, forced himself as far into her as it was possible for him to go. His face was an ugly, twisted, inhuman, mask, as he raised himself on his arms above her and let out a terrible scream of satisfaction. The only thing Justina was free to move was her head. She thrashed from side to side in fear, pain and desperation. Even with her clothes torn and her face bloody and bruised her body was

still beautiful. The perfume she had put on specially, drove them all just as mad with lust as it had driven Van Es. Atek roughly pushed the last man out of the way. The perfume was in his nostrils, the memory of her still fresh. He had to have her again!

Justina's body was whiter and cleaner than any woman's body he had ever seen. Her waist was small above her well proportioned hips. Her breasts delectably soft. For Atek, entering her thighs was like the coming home Van Es had always felt when he had made passionate love to her. Having her was like having a Dutch woman. Atek had seen many sexy white women but, even if they had cast an eye on him, natives were forbidden to have relationships with white women. The fact that a white woman was unattainable made the lust of men like Atek all the stronger. Looking at Justina now, lying vulnerably on her back, her arms helplessly above her head, her legs wide apart, as available as a woman could ever be, Atek felt that it was not a Eurasian but a white woman he was taking! A Dutch woman! A member of the arrogant, imperious, foreign, ruling class whom he hated as only the poor and dispossessed can hate!

Atek fell onto Justina again, tearing at her with his fingers, forcing himself inside. Justina hated all these men, feared them all. Her muscles had instinctively resisted them all. All had had to force themselves into her. Suddenly Atek resented this deeply. Even helpless on her back, Justina still had no time for him, still made it clear that he was beneath her, made having her as difficult and unpleasant as possible. She would open her legs to any

Dutchman any time, but not to him, an Inlander! Atek hated her with uncontrollable hatred. It gave him deep pleasure to know that he could hurt her as much as he liked without even the smallest fear of retribution. No one knew they were here. No one could see them or hear them. His mind and body craved revenge for all the insults he had ever suffered at the hands of the Dutch!

"You Dutch bitch," he hissed, with blazing eyes. "This is the last time you put down Atek."

Justina could hear the sound of carriages far away, now and again a shout. The leaves were thick above her head but here and there she could glimpse the dark, star studded sky. With all her heart she wished that by some magic spell she could be in one of the carriages, or be able to ask the shouters for help, or to be safe, high in the peaceful heavens. Anywhere, but trapped in the dirt like a trussed chicken while three reeking, foul breathed, black brutes ravaged and hurt her.

As he moved inside her, Atek clasped his hands tightly round Justina's lily-white neck, throttling her, banging her head up and down on the stony ground. Justina's eyes bulged. She no longer heard or saw anything. Her cheeks puffed rapidly in and out as she tried to squeeze even a small breath through the stifling wad in her mouth. All the time, Atek plunged mercilessly in and out of her until, when his body arched to its climax, the grip of his hands was at its tightest round Justina's slender throat. Justina's small, girl's body was no match for the ferocity of the attack. When Atek's passion begun to fade, when he withdrew from her and slacked his grip on her throat, Justina lay like a rag doll on the ground.

"Mati!" ("Dead!") a coarse voice said.

"Of course she's dead, idiot," growled Atek. What did you think would happen?"

Atek sent one of the men back to the coverless sado for a gunny sack which they drew over Justina's battered head before forcing her knees up under her chin and tying the thick bag tightly closed. Her eyes still bulged with pain and horror and the gag was still in her mouth. They brought the sado closer and dumped the sack carelessly in the back. Atek ordered the two men to dispose of the corpse and went about his business. It was not late and there were still carriages on the road. He warned the hoodlums to drive slowly so as not to attract any attention, especially passing through the lights and crowds of Senen. At last, Justina was out of the dark woods and among milling crowds and bright lights! But already she was far beyond any help! The killers did not have to drive far. East of Senen, the Kali Baru was lined with dense trees and shrubs, with here and there a path down to the canal. There were no buildings or people here and the two strong-arm men found a place where they could get close to the canal but not be seen. It was quick and light work to heave the pitifully small bag into the canal, where the black waters hid Justina from the world for the last time. The men were well satisfied. No one had seen them. The body was heavy enough to sink to the bottom of the canal. No one would ever find her. No one would ever know!

7

For the next few days, Van Es looked ap prehensively for Justina to turn up again at the villa, or to appear outside his office or, worse still, to be told that a woman answering her description was waiting for him in the office of the General! But Justina was never seen anywhere and nothing was heard from her. Van Es swept her from his thoughts as totally as if she had never been there, and settled into his new job, every day, deeply absorbed in studying what had to be done and issuing streams of orders. As Major Van Es, he had thought of himself as a glorified clerk but, as Colonel Van Es, he no longer spent long hours at his desk, albeit satisfyingly larger in a bigger of-fice. As a staff officer, there were many important meetings to attend and high level discussions in which to take part. Van Es became totally immersed in the military life and his new responsibilities.

He was so busy that he felt no interest in pursuing his night-life in Senen. He told himself that maybe now that phase of his life was over - or should be over. Colonel Hogendorp had been quite pointed in his comments about the merits of a white, Dutch, wife. Maybe it was time for Van Es to start looking seriously among the ever increasing numbers of white girls arriving in the Indies. He smiled to himself. If he got tired of her he could always go back to Senen for a mistress! His new Dutch wife would have no way of finding out!

In any case, Van Es thought it best to curtail his nocturnal excursions to Senen until he was certain that Atek had dealt with Justina and that the outcome was positive. He was frustrated at not being able to find out what had happened. Clearly, he could not just send for Atek or go to Atek's and ask. He could only wait. His arrangement with Atek was that, after Justina had been taught a lesson, Atek would find a way of contacting him for his second payment.

At Atek's, life went on as usual, accept that Siti missed her friend and asked everyone who knew Justina if they had seen her or had heard where she was. She could not ask Justina's family, because, although she counted Justina as a friend, she had never asked where she lived. In the kampong, Justina's family were mildly, but not seriously, worried because it was in the nature of Justina's profession that she should be out and about at odd times, sometimes for days and nights at a time.

With each passing day in which Van Es saw and heard nothing of Justina, he became more confident, his stride more deliberate and heavy, his orders more terse. Van Es knew that his promotion was exceptional but that he had been given it because he, too, was exceptional. He felt more and more exceptional the more used he became to being called "Colonel." He was secure, he was respected and, provided Justina didn't spoil everything by blabbing about their relationship, he was safe!

Van Es's passion for Justina had long ago evaporated, expunged by the ugly side of her which he felt she had shown him when he refused to marry her. As if a senior Dutch officer would ever would marry a common prostitute! Van Es rationalised that he had never loved Justina. She had pushed him to say he loved her! And he would have said that to any whore who pleased him! Of course, Justina had pleased him. Their love making had been fantastic. But it was not worth the price of marriage! If ever he felt the need to go to Senen again, there would be many lovely, passionate Indies girls to choose from. If he didn't take a Dutch wife, eventually, he would find another girl like Justina but next time he would not make the mistake of letting her stay the night! Once bitten, twice shy!

Van Es was now a member of another mess but, nevertheless, he found himself spending more time at the Concordia Club. It made him feel very grand to sweep up in a carriage and alight beneath the portico, with doormen running to help him out and salaam him within. Many an evening now, he took the opportunity to soak up the special atmosphere of the Concordia - its huge rooms, its heavy, carved wooden furniture, built locally to Dutch specifications, its gleaming gas lamps and chandeliers, its ornate stucco walls and painted ceilings and its mock Roman statues, all of which endowed the building with a sense of sophistication enjoyed by few of the Club's patrons - simple soldiers all.

The louvered green shutters on the long, narrow, windows were open throughout the day and, glancing through, Van Es always felt how appropriate it was for the Club to be situated cheek by jowl with the Dutch Indies Government's headquarters, with its statue of Batavia's founder, Jan Pieterszoon Coen on a high pedestal in front. Over there, they formed policy and made laws but, over here, at the Club, were the enforcers without whom those policies and laws would be meaningless. What an extraordinary privilege it was, thought Van Es, that he should now be a full Colonel at the very centre of Dutch power in the Indies.

For some unaccountable reason, what an extraordinary shock it was when he read in the 'Batavia News' that a young girl's body had been fished out of the Kali Baru. Tension immediately gripped Van Es's neck and a prickly heat broke out on his face.

A gang of young boys splashing about in the canal had found the sack containing Justina's body! The waters that had seemed to close so finally over her head, suddenly yielded her up to rejoin the world! The police had been called and the mutilated corpse taken away to the public mortuary.

Van Es's hands shook as he head the story. Suppose Atek had had to go all the way and kill

Justina to shut her up? Suppose the body found was really hers? Suppose, by some incredible chance, Justina was linked to him?

He pushed his anxieties rapidly aside by focusing on his status and power so that his eventual response to the nagging questions was: "So what!"

In reality, he had truthfully not killed Justina! Even if it was suspected that she died at his order what Dutchman would believe it? Even if it was proved that she died at his order what Dutchman would want to punish one of their own senior officers for doing to one Inlander the sort of thing they did to many, every day, in the jungle wars against rebels. And she was a prostitute to boot. The lowest of the low. He, on the other hand, was a Tuan besar, a man of proven, outstanding value and importance. No sane Dutchman would be willing to balance the worthless life of a whore with that of a full colonel!

Anyway, the body might not even be that of Justina! So, why worry?

Word had spread fast through the Inlander community that a dead person had been found. Justina's sculptured, woman's body was not in an advanced state of decay, but still recognisable. Police surgeons examined and catalogued her brutal injuries and confirmed her pregnancy. An announcement was quickly made that a young, pregnant, Eurasian woman had been found in the Kali Baru, battered mercilessly to death. Such an announcement had little affect in the kampongs, where the Inlanders usually kept well away from authority. But, the news very soon reached the ears of the girls in the night spots of Senen.

When Siti heard, she went numb with fear. Some sixth sense told her that the body was that of her friend, Justina.

When days passed and Justina had failed to show up at Atek's, Siti feared the worst. Knowing where her friend lived she had taken the trouble to go to Justina's house to try to see her. It hardly came as a surprise to her to hear that none of the family had seen Justina since she had gone off to keep her secret tryst with Van Es! Justina's grandmother rocked silently backwards and forwards as she sat on the matter floor, her toothless gums clamped together grimly, her cheeks hollow. Her mother sat with downcast eyes, nervously picking and unpicking stray ends of the same mat. Her sisters looked frightened. Among the sad and silent waiters there was an atmosphere of normal life having been suspended under the dark shadow of some terrible impending tragedy. Siti did not want to worry and frighten them further by telling about the body in the canal but she hurried to Atek's to voice her suspicions. Atek told her brusquely that such an event was none of their business.

"It's best for people like us to keep well out of happenings like this," he almost snarled.

Siti couldn't rest until she knew. If the body wasn't Justina's, where was Justina? The fact that Justina was missing just at the same moment that a young woman's body was discovered in a canal near Senen gave her no rest. She had to find out. Maybe the only way was to ask the police. But she could not go alone to a police station! Anything could happen to her. She told her fears to some other working girls and begged them to go with her to the police.

"We can't, we can't, they had said initially. "He is a Tuan besar. Little people like us have no chance against a belanda Tuan besar. It will be we who get into trouble, not him."

But, loyalty to her friend drove Siti to persist until she wore them down and convinced them that they had to go with her. At the police barracks, they were frightened and shy and had no idea where to go or who to ask. Shuffling and fidgeting nervously they finally managed to explain disjointedly that a girl called Justina was their friend and that she had disappeared. Big, wet, tears flowed down Siti's cheeks when she forced herself to say that they feared the body recently found dumped in the canal might be Justina's.

The police had no clues or leads and seized eagerly upon the girls in case they really could identify the body. None of them had ever seen a dead body before and the thought of it made them all more nervous still. They made a pitiful little group as they walked, with heads bowed down, behind the officers escorting them to the morgue. A door was opened and, before them, in the big, empty, room, they could make out the shape of a body lying on a long, narrow, table.

"There's no need to look at the whole body," an officer told them. "She's been badly beaten and it will upset you. Even her face has been mutilated but you must try to look if we are to have any hope of identifying her."

The girls stepped timidly forward, forming a

little knot at one end of the sheet-covered table. Their little hearts pounded with fright. Slowly, the officer lifted the sheet. Each girl looked away before she had seen anything, so great was their terror. Finally, the sheet was turned far enough back and each girl forced herself to look once and then look away, hand over her mouth. One girl ran from the room retching terribly. Siti stood wide-eyed and weeping, her mouth open with gusting, choking, sobs, tears streaming down her face at the sight of her poor, battered, friend, her beauty virtually reduced to a mess of tissue and bone. There was no doubt; it was Justina!

The girls were led away but had to rest a while before any of them could speak, the horror of Justina's injuries vivid in their minds. Siti's black eyes burned with hatred, flamed with vengeance. She alone knew exactly who had committed this terrible crime! Had she not seen him, with her own eyes, in Atek's garden, with his hands round Justina's little throat.

"I know who killed her," she blurted out, suddenly courageous in the necessity of avenging her friend.

The police officers quizzed and questioned her. What did she know? How did she know it? What was the name of the killer."

"Van Es," Siti told them, "Colonel Hugo Van Es!"

Siti was warned that her allegation was extremely serious and that, for her own good, she had better not make any false charge. But Siti was adamant! She <u>had</u> seen Van Es attack Justina. Now

Justina had turned up dead! Who else could have killed her? Who else might have wanted her dead?

Siti's allegation put the matter way out of the hands of officers at this level, and the case was quickly and urgently referred to the Chief Superintendent of Police, Meneer Schenkenburg.

Schenkenberg was predictably outraged.

"How dare an Inlander make such an allegation," he roared, his face red. "Colonel Van Es is one of our most respected officers. Bring the girl to me. I'll soon get the truth out of her."

Siti now had all the courage in the world! As far as she was concerned they could do to her what they liked! She had told the truth before and she told it again now!

After Siti had repeated her story several times, told him how Justina used to stay At Van Es's villa, how they had quarrelled and what about, Schenkenberg sighed with deep and genuine distress - not for Justina, but for Van Es!

Officers had been writing down what Siti had been saying and, finally, a paper with words on it was read to her and she was asked to confirm that this was what she had said.

"Yes, that's what I said," she agreed quietly.

Schenkenburg asked her to put her mark at the bottom of the paper and told her that she was free to go.

"This case is going to be very difficult," he muttered to himself irritably, instructing all who knew about it to keep quiet and tell no one until the true facts were known.

Before the day had ended, many, many people

knew that an Inlander had accused a high Dutch official of murdering a beautiful prostitute. And before the day had ended the worst of Van Es's fears were realised, not by receiving a call from the General, but by his adjutant informing him apologetically that Police Chief Superintendent Schenkenburg was in the outer office requesting to see him! Van Es's hands shook more. His tension rose. If he knew his role in punishing Justina, the whole world must surely know it! He felt as if his very guilt was emblazoned across his face for everyone to see.

The Superintendent was embarrassed and begged Van Es's pardon for troubling him with something which was bound to be untrue!

Van Es listened to the charge and, suppressing his inner fears and feelings, huffed and puffed in feigned outrage.

But the Superintendent was not merely a fellow Dutchman, a fellow officer; he was also a good policeman. Like Van Es, he too dreamed of promotion and promotion could only be earned by doing a good job!

Van Es was stumblingly forced to own that he had been seeing Justina.

"So what. Everybody is entitled to a girl friend," he laughed with unusual loudness.

Schenkenburg edged Van Es to admit that he had quarrelled with Justina in Atek's garden. But, the Colonel denied categorically that he had ever put his hands to her throat. Knowing the unlikelihood of colonial officials taking a native's word against a Dutchman's, he also denied that she had ever stayed with him at the villa.

Schenkenburg assured him that he believed him totally and repeated again and again that it must all be an unfortunate misunderstanding. While he listened, Schenkenburg divulged nothing of his future intentions to Van Es. It came as a complete surprise when Van Es reached home for his late afternoon siesta that Supardi informed him that the police had been to the villa and searched it thoroughly!

"Outrageous, Absolutely outrageous", growled Van Es irritably. "The civil police have no authority over me and no business here." He slammed into his bedroom and shut himself in. "The police! Here!" At first his heart raced but, once again, he rationalised. "What if they had searched the house? What could they find to link him to Justina? Nothing! Absolutely nothing!"

Van Es had little idea of how wrong he was! The native police and their European officer had not only searched but asked Supardi many questions. His answers enabled them to arrive at a complete picture of Van Es's true relationship with Justina. Most damning of all, Supardi was able to produce Justina's sarong, that, in a rage, Van Es had told him to burn! Van Es's assertion that Justina had never stayed at the villa was immediately exposed as a lie!

Supadi felt that Justina had always been kind to him, had never sought to displace him from Van Es's service, and had worked with him to serve and please their joint master. Though he knew she looked down on Inlanders and thought herself a Nyonya besar (grand lady), nevertheless Supardi had also fallen under the spell of her fragile beauty. His dark eyes had been sad with grief for her since he had heard the news of her murder. He could see her still in his mind's eye, exploring the rooms of the little house, buying from vendors, working with him to make delicious meals, sometimes even sharing with him some of the money he knew Van Es gave her. Whatever status her profession gave her in society, Supadi felt that she was a lady because she had always treated him fairly and had never shouted at him or abused him. Certainly, such a sweet girl did not deserve to die. Certainly, no Dutchman, however high, should be allowed to kill her and get away with it. After all, whoever Justina, herself, thought she was, at root she was one of <u>his</u> people, her killer a foreign interloper!

Supadi had asked permission to fetch Justina's sarong, still smelling of her seductive perfume. Before handing it over, Supadi pressed the folded sarong to his face for one last time, as he had done many a night in his little, bare, servant's room. He could never have dreamed of having a woman like her!

Next day, Superintendent Schenkenburg visited Van Es again. This time he brought with him the sarong and this time Van Es was forced to admit that, since it was not his practice to allow prostitutes to stay in his villa, he had inadvertently forgotten that Justina had stayed there "once or twice."

The time came when Schenkenburg looked him straight in the eyes and asked him calmly:

"Did you kill this girl," Colonel Van Es.

"Absolutely not," exploded Van Es, confident

in the knowledge that he had not! "Even though I admit I quarrelled with her I would be the last person to kill her!"

Of course, there was no proof that Van Es had killed Justina. All the evidence was circumstantial. The police had proved that he had been seeing her, that she had stayed at his villa and that he had quarrelled with her. But she had been seen alive after the quarrel so, if Van Es had killed her, it had to have been at another time or else someone else was the killer! Who that might be was anybody's guess!

The police were stonewalled. The case-file lay unopened and gathering dust in a pending tray!

Through Siti, Justina's family had been located and informed, and arrangements had quickly been made for a simple funeral - the only kind they could afford! On the day of the funeral, there were not many to escort Justina to her final resting place and only a small knot of mourners set out from the house, Justina's coffin borne before them on the shoulders of male neighbours. But the story of Justina's death had become known to everyone in the kampong and as the little procession passed slowly by more and more people followed until, by the time they reached the cemetery, there was a throng of several hundred people!

At the graveside, her mother and grandmother sobbed uncontrollably, repeatedly shaking their heads at the thought of Justina brushing aside their warnings and insisting to meet a dangerous belanda like Van Es, and then ending up like this! Such a beautiful girl! Such a waste! Justina's sisters' faces were tortured with pain as they stood beside their hysterical elders, virtually propping them up. When the priest voiced the hope that Justina's killer would be caught and punished the large crowd murmured angrily.

"He is a Dutchman. He will not be punished," a man shouted.

The crowd's murmur turned to a roar of objection. A few of them knew Justina, but, even the many who didn't, felt instinctively that she was one of them and that one of their own had been unfairly and brutally murdered by one of the greedy, insensitive, Dutch invaders. One comment inspired another, speaker inflamed speaker until the crowd was howling for justice. Police were summoned but, at the sight of the uniforms, stones began to be thrown, so that reinforcements had to be called. The more the police tried to control the crowd, the larger the mob became, until a pitched battle was being raged at the cemetery and in the surrounding streets. Small groups broke away and stoned and smashed windows of any Dutch buildings they could find. The frustrated crowd did not disperse until well after dark.

Learning of the riot, Schenkenburg was not the only one to have a renewed sense that Justina's killer must be caught and punished. Many in the Government felt that the reaction of the crowd was a sign of the times! Increasingly, the natives were docile no more!

Atek, meanwhile, had been irritated at being unable to find Van Es to recover the second half of his payment. Van Es had not thought to inform him that he was moving office and, of course, had not been back to Senen. Atek sent one of his men to loiter about and enquire after Van Es's whereabouts from low level local staff. While it was easy to locate his new office it was extremely difficult to be allowed in! Yet he had to get in to see Van Es if he was ever to get paid! Atek could think of no reason for requesting to meet with Van Es that security guards would be believe. Several times, he hung about, outside the gates into Van Es's compound hoping to see him but, unluckily, he never even glimpsed Van Es. He bribed someone to tell him the exact position of Van Es's office within its compound to see how close to it he could get, but the office faced inwards onto an inner quadrangle with no doors or windows accessible to anyone outside. Atek was stymied! What to do? Something had to be done! He spent days watching people coming and going, trying to work out when was a quiet time so that he could try to sneak directly to Van Es's office. Eventually, by some miracle, he succeeded in getting all the way in, undetected. He reached out to open Van Es's door. Abruptly he heard rushing feet and he was seized from behind by guards.

"What are you doing here," they shouted. "You filthy dog. Don't you know that this compound is closed. Don't you know that this is the office of a Tuan besar."

Atek's appearance was all against him. His face was very black, with an evil, downward drooping pencil moustache. His wide trousers ended just below the knee, his batik top was dirty and, alarmingly, a dagger was found in his belt.

"What are you doing here? What do you want? Were you going to kill someone with this knife?" the guards shouted contemptuously and threateningly. "If you don't tell us you'll be put under arrest!

Atek was frightened! He was trapped! Above all he had to get away. He blurted out:

"Colonel Van Es owes me some money for supplies and I have come to get it, that's all!"

"A likely story," the guards sneered. Colonel Van Es would not himself pay directly to someone like you. You're lying. Why are you lying? What are you trying to hide?"

"He asked me to do a job for him," Atek snivelled. "But he never paid me."

The military guards were now seriously interested. What possible job could scum like Atek have carried out for a Tuan besar such as Colonel Van Es! Atek knew it was useless to struggle and allowed himself to be marched away for questioning. The questioners began with the obvious: "Name, address, occupation?" There was no need to go further! Once it was realised that Atek was the owner of a virtual brothel in Senen, it was also known that his was the very bawdy house frequented by the murdered prostitute, a murder of which Colonel Van Es was suspected, the very man Atek was trying to meet!

Unfortunately for Atek, the guards he had stumbled into were Eurasian. At headquarters, the Dutch liked to surround themselves with Eurasians, partly because of their enhanced abilities to undertake support work and partly because of their supposed racial loyalty.

The guards already knew all about Justina's

foul murder. If she belonged to any group, she belonged to theirs! Harming her was the same as harming them. They well knew the hopes, fears and insecurities of Eurasian people, particularly with the growing flood of pure Dutch arriving weekly from Holland. They had heard about the threatening new regulation, forbidding officers to take up with local women, including girls of mixed race.

They had also heard that Justina had been good to Colonel Van Es, was carrying his child and wanted to marry him. Nothing thrived so well in Batavia as gossip and every detail of Van Es's relationship with Justina was passed from mouth to mouth in ever widening circles. The beautiful Eurasian girl was consistently portrayed as an innocent and helpless victim. The Eurasians were fighting to maintain their position in colonial society and no attack on any one of them could be allowed to pass unheeded. Despite their traditional loyalty to their white masters, the eyes of the Eurasians glinted at the thought of Van Es throwing her out of his house into the street! Their eyes positively blazed with anger at the thought that the Colonel might really be Justina's killer!

Their suspicions fully aroused, the guards determined to squeeze the truth out of Atek. For a few hours, the brothel owner disappeared! When he was seen next he was bloody and staggering and it was clear from the expressions on the faces of the accompanying police that Atek had been very talkative!

Chief Superintendent Schenkenburg read Atek's 'confession' with great sadness. There was no longer any doubt. Van Es had ordered and paid for the death of an Indies woman! True, he had not killed her himself, but giving the order amounted to the same thing! Colonel Van Es would have to be interviewed again! Or would he? Superintendent Schenkenburg realised that the end of this case was in sight but there was a problem. Van Es was a military officer and not subject to the authority of the police! Schenkenberg knew that he must now refer the tragedy to the military police and, accordingly, made an appointment with police Colonel Bosveld. When they met, the case was virtually open and shut. All that remained was to decide what step to take next!

Bosveld decided that the advice must be sought from General Van des Velden before further action was taken.

Van des Velden was shocked and, for a while, leant back stunned in his chair.

"Such an outstanding officer," he sighed. "Such a pity."

Van des Velden knew all about the cemetery riot and was as clued-in as any politician to the rising tide of nascent nationalism in parts of the Indies, especially Java.

"In this case, Justice must take its course," he told Colonel Bosveld without hesitation.

For a split second the blue eyes of the two men met, Van des Velden's cold and expressionless, Bosveld's probing to leave no room for doubt.

Bosveld collected an armed escort and made for Colonel Van Es's office. The Colonel was not there but as they were marching across an open parade ground he came towards them, walking proudly, swinging his arms. He did not know Bosveld and walked purposely forward.

"Colonel Van Es," called Bosveld.

"Yes, you want me?"

"I have some bad news for you Colonel."

Van Es's heart almost stopped beating!

"Bad news?"

Even without looking, he sensed guards up positions behind and on either side of him.

"Colonel Van Es," Bosveld continued. "I arrest you for complicity in the murder of Miss Justina Oostenbroek!"

Van Es was shocked to hear the prostitute Justina described so respectfully. As usual, tension gripped him immediately, tightening his throat and neck muscles. But he still managed a contemptuous reaction.

"This must be a joke. I've been all through this with the civil police. I didn't kill her," shouted Van Es. "Why don't you go out and find the real killer instead of harassing me?"

"You must come along with us Colonel. Everything will be explained to you later," said Bosveld.

"This is an outrage," shouted Van Es. "I demand to see the General. Wait 'till he hears about this. I am a Colonel in the Netherlands Indies forces. You can't arrest me like a common thief."

"We are not arresting you for theft," said Bosveld dryly.

Van Es felt soldiers touch his arms lightly and knew that they would grab him instantly if he tried to break away.

Van Es thought he would be taken to the military police compound but, instead, he saw that they were marching in the direction of Colonel Hogendorp's office.

Hogendorp looked grim and made no effort either at small talk or any other kind of talk. He let Van Es stand uneasily in front of his desk, guards on either side. He nodded at Colonel Bosveld.

"If you please Colonel."

Bosveld opened a side door and the battered and pitiful figure of Atek was led in!

Van Es drew in his breath.

"You!"

"Ma'af" (Sorry), Tuan," mumbled Atek, his head bent downwards and his eyes lowered.

Van Es flew forward, his hands grabbing at Atek's throat, but while the native fell to the floor the guards held Van Es fast.

"I think you have answered all the questions I had, Colonel," said Hogendorp. "Good day to you."

Van Es knew that the game was up! They had him! He was locked in a cell overnight where he had plenty of time to weigh up his plight. Was it really so bad? What could they really do to him. What would they be prepared to do? How far would they want to proceed against one of their own, a senior Dutch officer? And, after all, the fact was that he had not killed Justina. Those were not his hands at her throat; they were Atek's. So, what would happen. Would there be a court martial? Would he be tried? If found guilty what would the punishment be? A halt to further promotion? A re-posting to some frontier hell-hole? It would be bitter not to be able to advance further he told himself but a hell-hole he could tolerate, for a short time! The killing, and his part in it, would soon be forgotten and he might pop up again, covered in glory for his exploits in crushing the government's enemies in the jungles of the islands.

Very early next morning, Bosweld came to see him and Van Es immediately took the chance to ask what was going to happen to him next.

"There will be a court martial, Colonel."

Van Es had anticipated this and was, therefore, not surprised.

"I understand," he said in a conversational tone, as if they were discussing one of his beloved procedures.

"What do you think will happen to me?"

"I have no idea, Colonel. It will be for the court to decide. By the way Colonel Hogendorp is coming to see you this afternoon."

"Oh, yes! About what.

"I really don't know Colonel. The Colonel did not confide in me."

Van Es sensed that the winds were about to change and ate a hearty lunch in good spirits.

"Of course," something will happen," he told himself. "The Government is not going to sacrifice a talented young colonel for a common prostitute!"

When Hogendorp arrived he looked uncustomarily grim. He asked his escort to wait on the other side of the cell door, which he closed partially to prevent them hearing what was being said.

"Van Es," he said, slightingly omitting the Colonel's new title.

"I want you to know what is going to happen to you."

"I have already been told, thank you, Sir."

"I doubt that you have. Listen to me now. There is to be a court martial and, from the evidence I don't doubt that you will be found guilty."

Van Es remained calm. There was nothing new in this.

"In the Indies today we are facing a serious upsurge of demands from the native people. They want more from us. They want to be treated what they call fairly. Already, even in the normal course of events, groups are meeting and discussing their wants, their demands. Any day, such meetings could turn into plots against the Netherlands Indies Government. We cannot afford to fuel this process by appearing to be lenient with you. I don't know if you are aware of it but, at this girl's funeral the other day we had a riot on our hands!"

Van Es stared at him. He was no longer calm. Alarm bells were ringing in his head!

"Lenient?" he queried.

"I am bound to tell you, Van Es, that I think your sentence will not merely be to be disgraced. Of course, you will be paraded at Koningsplein, stripped of your medal, your buttons and braids cut off, your epaulettes slashed - and you will be discharged.

Van Es swallowed hard. Disgrace! Discharge! Such things would be unbearable!

"But, I don't think the punishment will or can end there," Hogendorp continued.

Van Es stared at him again, wide eyed. What other punishment could there possibly be?

"I think that the court will sentence you to death!"

Van Es's brain was numb. His face twitched. His lips trembled. His fists clenched and unclenched. tension welled up around his neck as if to choke him.

"Death!"

"You are a Dutch officer. You have ordered the unjust death of a Eurasian. The Netherlands Indies Government cannot be seen to support such a vile act. Indeed, we must make it very plain that we condemn it utterly."

"But she was a common whore," spluttered Van Es in exasperation, forgetting all military protocol in the extremity of his situation, "she was worthless, a woman of absolutely no account!"

"She was a living, breathing, human being, Colonel. And you had her cold-bloodedly killed!"

Van Es was in shock, his face white. He collapsed onto a wooden stool in the corner of the small cell.

"Of course, Colonel," Hogendorp went on, "the government and the army could be saved a lot of embarrassment."

Van Es looked up at him with watery eyes.

"As a senior officer, if you were to do the honourable thing, the details of this case need never be made public. We don't want a case dragging on in full public view during which the colonial government will be perpetually vilified. There is still a way of redeeming your honour. Think about it Colonel!"

On this menacing note Hogendorp left Van Es alone!

All afternoon Van Es agonised, tried to identify a way out. He saw himself once again at Koningsplein, receiving his promotion and medal in front of the assembled ranks of flag-flying, drum-beating, imperial troops. Looking back, the whole thing seemed like a dream. Within two days he had fallen from being Colonel Hugo Van Es to an incarcerated criminal under sentence of death! For once, he was in a straight-jacket with absolutely no options! In the frighteningly near future, the grand career he had mapped out for himself would be snuffed out with his life!

Death terrified him beyond words. He could bear disgrace but death! Who but a complete idiot could welcome death! The Tuan besar who had planned to make his name killing rebellious natives went hot at the thought of being killed himself! Gradually, terror worked him up to a near-insane anger in which he ranted and raved and cursed and shook the sturdy bars of his cell. It was hours before he calmed down and sat slumped in a corner, dribbling from his mouth. But then a demented gleam came into his eyes. If he was going to die, Colonel Van Es would do it in his own way and in his own time. If there could be no other, suicide, at least, would be the most glorious act of his life! He regretted nothing about Justina and there was no way he was going to let other people say he was wrong by imposing their punishment on him. He would punish them by taking his own life! It was they who would be sorry, not Van Es! In his mind, the drums beat and the trumpets blared, as they had at Koningsplein; he would meet his death at the charge, with a battle cry of defiance! This was Hugo Van Es!

At dead of night, with a great, orange, moon, illuminating his cell, Van Es slipped off his belt and hooked it over an exposed iron girder in the low ceiling. He stood on the top of the cell's single wooden stool and painstakingly tied the end of the belt round his neck. He would show them the stuff Van Es was made of! No disgrace for him! No dishonourable discharge! No ignominious death in front of a firing squad! Van Es felt buoyed with the image of it all; a tough Dutch officer courageously giving the finger to the world.

A determined and decisive man would have knotted the belt and kicked over the stool immediately but, at the thought of the finality of doing it, instead, he stood for a long time, looking at the moon, temporising! Should he do it or shouldn't he? Was there still a way out or wasn't there? Finally, he decided there wasn't and used his boot to angrily begin slowly tipping over the stool, the right side dipping down as it toppled, the left side rising up. He toed the stool gently, almost as if he didn't mean to do it, as if he still yet might pull back. Van Es felt the belt tighten round his throat! Felt himself unable to swallow! Felt himself begin to choke! Panic and cowardice took over! He decided he couldn't do it and that he would quickly tilt the stool upright again simply by blocking the rising left side with his boot. But the boot was leather, smooth as glass! He felt his foot touching the stool but sliding past. He panicked. In a millisecond he knew he was going to die! Shockingly, jarringly, the full weight of his heavy body plunged downwards with a neck breaking jerk, the leather belt tightening round his neck. But his neck was not broken and Van Es hung there, his fingers tearing vainly at the belt, ever tightening around his throat. Like Justina, Van Es's eyes bulged from their sockets and, like her, he died there choking in his own spit!

There was no funeral for Van Es, no eulogy, no kind words, no relatives even. His body was hastily burned and his ashes scattered so that no trace of his existence remained! His dress uniform was ripped up at Koningsplein, before a parade of all units stationed at Batavia, exactly as if he had been wearing it. His ceremonial sword was broken in two and thrown contemptuously on the ground where cavalry later rode over it!.

Hugo Van Es had come East to help 'tame' and triumph over the Indies, without a care about whether what he did was right or wrong, moral or immoral. But, the unquenchable determination of the people of the Indies to be treated fairly was so strong that, even from the very grave itself, Justina's spirit, the spirit of the Indies, had reached out from her trampled body to triumph over <u>him</u>!

Other fiction and historical tourism publications by Richard Mann

A Clown On The Streets of Jakarta

A Hardship Post

Restless Warrior - Sir Thomas Stamford Raffles

The Old City Of Jakarta - TODAY